Fifty Shades of Gay

Jeffery Self is a writer and an actor. He co-created and starred in *Jeffery and Cole Casserole* on Logo and has appeared on numerous television shows, including *Desperate Housewives, 90210, Hot in Cleveland* and *30 Rock* as Randy Lemon. His book *Straight People: A Spotter's Guide* is forthcoming. Follow him on Twitter @JefferySelf. You can also visit him online at Jefferyself.tumblr.com.

Fifty Shades of Gay

JEFFERY SELF

HarperCollins *Publishers* India

First published in India in 2014 by
HarperCollins *Publishers* India

P-ISBN: 978-93-5136-972-1
E-ISBN: 978-93-5136-973-8

2 4 6 8 10 9 7 5 3 1

HarperCollins *Publishers*
A-75, Sector 57, Noida, Uttar Pradesh 201301, India
77-85 Fulham Palace Road, London W6 8JB, United Kingdom
Hazelton Lanes, 55 Avenue Road, Suite 2900, Toronto, Ontario M5R 3L2 and 1995 Markham Road, Scarborough, Ontario M1B 5M8, Canada
25 Ryde Road, Pymble, Sydney, NSW 2073, Australia
10 East 53rd Street, New York NY 10022, USA

Typeset in 10.5/14.5 Sabon by
R. Ajith Kumar

Printed and bound at
Replika Press Pvt. Ltd.

To Jacqueline Susann, whose books continue to teach me just how glamorous filth can be.

CHAPTER 1

'CAN YOU DO ME a huge favour?' Matty asks, poking his head into my bedroom and looking paler than LaToya Jackson with a stomach virus.

Matty has never been shy about asking for favours. That's the territory that comes with being roommates and best friends for four years, the expectation of favours. Like having a boyfriend you can depend on, but without the sex, intimate connection or expensive birthday gifts. My favours for Matty have run the gamut from 4 a.m. airport drop-offs to plucking some really unfortunately placed back hairs before we went to Gay Days at Disney World, which led to even more favours, the weirdest of which involved my driving Matty and the eerily youthful-looking thirty-five-year-old man who played Peter Pan to what would later become the worst date in Matty's dating history. So I'd learnt years ago to brace myself when those words came out of Matty's mouth: 'Can you do me a huge favour?'

I pause the episode of *The Real Housewives of I-don't-even-know-where*, and answer a tentative 'Sure.'

'It's a work thing, so I'll throw you forty bucks.'

This is a relief to hear, and not just because it involves forty bucks—although I could certainly use that, as I am currently living off cater waiter gigs I've found on Craigslist. More importantly, however, Matty works as a reporter for a very popular entertainment show called *The Star Report*. They're like *Entertainment Tonight*, except more popular and without Billy Bush's uncomfortable energy.

I'm an aspiring writer myself and this wouldn't be the first time I've covered something for Matty. I wrote a really positive review of the movie *New Year's Eve*, which went kind of viral because it was literally the only positive review of *New Year's Eve*. What can I say? I've got a soft spot for movies about the holidays and Robert De Niro in hospital beds. Besides that, my professional writing experience has, up until now, been limited to a blog I kept during my first year living here in Los Angeles that, as of today, still has only twenty views. One of these days, however, I'm going to write a book.

'Sure. What is it?' I ask, hoping he'll say the two words I'm basically always waiting to hear: Meryl Streep.

'I'm scheduled to go to the press junket for this new Taylor Grayson movie. It's called *The Last* ...' He continues, but I've stopped listening. Taylor Grayson is one of the most beautiful movie stars in the history of beautiful movie stars. In fact, *People* magazine has ranked him 'Sexiest Man Alive' every year since I was a freshman in college and he was playing one on TV. Matty continues explaining the favour, but I'm lost in thought, remembering that scene from *The Yard*, a movie where he played a talented college football player who did something important that I can't remember. What I *can* remember is that I spent the whole movie replaying his four-minute shower scene, where steamy close-ups show tiny beads of hot water dripping down a perfectly tanned six-pack Michelangelo couldn't have carved if he'd tried, and a thirty-second shot of his gorgeous round butt that may or may not have been paused on my DVD player for most of 2009.

'So will you do it?' Matty asks, his story apparently finished. I look up at him, not having heard a word he said, and reply, 'Sure.'

Matty looks at me closely, the way he always looks at me when he knows I've not been listening. It's almost as if he's trying to look into my soul, but in actuality I know he's really just thinking, 'Why doesn't this asshole ever listen to a word I say?'

'Okay, cool. So you'll need rubber rain boots, a machete, and about three and a half feet of knitting yarn,' Matty says, nonchalantly.

'Sorry. I wasn't listening. I got distracted.'

Matty rolls his eyes and explains the situation. *The Star Report* is scheduled to interview Taylor Grayson about his new movie *The Last Hero* at a press junket at the Beverly Hills Hotel. It's a standard junket interview: reporter comes in, has four minutes to ask a series of approved vague questions, then leaves. Matty is supposed to go, but because he's come down with a stomach flu, he needs a replacement and no one else from the blog is available.

I remind Matty that I've never done on-camera interviewing before, or anything on camera for that matter ... unless you count the videotape of my exceedingly underwhelming performance as Tevye in my high school production of *Fiddler on the Roof*— which, for the record, I do not.

As usual, Matty's perception of my ability is a lot better than my own. Matty has a way of being so confident in people that it almost seems offensive, like, 'How dare you think I am *that* smart? Haven't you listened to a word I've ever said? Don't you know me at all?'

'You'll be great. All you have to do is be excited to talk to the star and excited to talk about the movie. Both of which you can handle. Need I remind you it is Taylor Grayson? I'm *sure* you can muster up some enthusiasm for *him.*'

Matty has a point. It wouldn't be hard to get excited over Taylor Grayson. For one, he would be the most famous person I've ever met, and two, I'm already getting aroused just thinking about him.

'What would I ask?' is the next question I direct to Matty, attempting to steer the subject away from anything having to do with the way Taylor Grayson's biceps seem to stretch out every shirt sleeve he wears to what must be the verge of ripping out completely.

'Standard press junket questions ... What was the hardest part of making the movie? Why did you take this role? Who was your inspiration for the character ... he plays a firefighter, by the way.'

I nod, as if I'm hearing about this for the first time. It isn't that I'm some psycho Taylor Grayson stalker by any means, far from it ... but I'd be lying if I claimed I hadn't masturbated, on multiple occasions, to the moment in his new movie trailer where he does something like forty pull-ups without taking a break. Taylor Grayson is a lot of things to America—internationally beloved movie star, magazine cover model, tabloid favourite—but most of all he's a member of just about every gay man's and straight woman's 'spank bank'.

'So will you do it?' Matty asks me with a look that combines the eyes of a sad puppy and the face of someone wanting you to do their job for them.

How often, I think to myself, does one come face to face with one of his ultimate sexual fantasies? Sure, I live in Los Angeles, but it's still not every day. I saw Brad Pitt in a Trader Joe's once, and I still talk about it at dinner parties ... and, to be honest, I'm not even a hundred per cent sure it was Brad Pitt. At the very least, this face-to-face, this one-on-one with Taylor Grayson could be just that—wonderful dinner party conversation.

I worry, for a moment, about the age old advice: 'Never meet your idols.' But Taylor Grayson isn't my idol, he's just someone I find very hot. Very, very insanely, drop-dead, getting-hard-even-thinking-about-him hot. Without a second thought or a single doubt in my head, I answer an immediate and eager: 'Yes.'

CHAPTER 2

IT ISN'T UNTIL I'M in the car, driving over to the Beverly Hills Hotel, that I realize just how weird what I'm doing is. Wednesday afternoons at the Beverly Hills Hotel are hardly in my life's usual repertoire. Neither is Beverly Hills itself for that matter. I've probably been to Beverly Hills only twice—once to see Rodeo Drive when I first moved to California and the second time when I got lost on my way to the Beverly Center and almost hit the woman who played the wife on *Home Improvement* with my car.

I'm increasingly nervous and I don't know why. It can't be just the overwhelming pressure that comes from entering the 90210 zip code. This is a bigger kind of nervous, a stomach-so-tied-in-knots-I-couldn't-finish-my-granola kind of nervous, and there's something else, something a bit less familiar. It's an excitement, a tentative sense of adventure. I tell myself to calm down, to not overthink it. I turn up the radio to full blast. It's Katy Perry singing 'Firework', and like any self-respecting homosexual, I can't help but sing along. I feel good. Not quite a firework but maybe a ... scented candle?

The feeling doesn't last for long as I pull onto Sunset Boulevard—I'm met with an enormous billboard of none other than Taylor Grayson himself staring down at the cars passing by. He's in a dark plaid suit with a perfectly fitted white shirt, unbuttoned just a few buttons below decent, and he's glaring into the camera with a smouldering, mysterious, oddly serious and beyond sexy look. The pants hug his thighs in a way that no pants have ever hugged thighs before. Most of the time, I don't fall for this kind of overt attempt to sell something based solely on the look of the person wearing it. I'm not one of those guys who melts at the drop of a hat, or towel in the gym, but there's something about this towering Taylor Grayson picture that sends a feeling from my stomach down to between my legs and suddenly I'm sweating.

I crack the window open and a woman next to me in traffic gives me a dirty look. I've forgotten just how loud I've turned my radio and before I can grab the volume control the woman shouts, 'We get it! You're a firework!' and flips me the bird. Welcome to Los Angeles.

Four minutes, I tell myself, repeating these words in my head, four minutes, that is all the time it will take to get this interview in the can. I haven't been this nervous since I tried my hand at dating and that was, what, three years ago? Dating was fun. Or rather the idea of dating was fun, but the actual act was ... depressing.

I met a handful of nice guys and a handful of cute guys, but none who were both. Los Angeles is quite possibly the worst place in America to try dating. People are either too ambitious to even learn your name unless you work for a big shot agency or so lazy that the majority of their time is spent smoking pot and watching old episodes of *Roseanne*. I belong, generally speaking, to the latter.

It's not that I'm not interested in men. I am. Men take up about seventy per cent of my thoughts, the other thirty made up of dreaming of Pinkberry and traveling to Paris someday (in that order). It's just that Los Angeles is a little outside my comfort zone, dating-wise. I love it here, but no matter how long I stay I just can't seem to get the courage to really *live*.

Which is code for: I'm a virgin. Yep. My name is Alex Kirby and I'm the last gay twenty-four-year-old virgin on earth. I came out kind of late or, at least, late for my generation. I was twenty. Even then it was basically forced out of me by Matty, who's been gay, as he puts it, since Jennifer Aniston had her first nose. It's not that I have a problem with being gay, I don't. I just grew up in the type of family that didn't like talking about feelings and certainly never uttered the word 'sex'.

We were Jehovah's Witnesses, and I'm still not sure what that means other than that we didn't celebrate holidays and I owned a three-piece suit from the age of five. My family taught us that any kind of even remotely sexual thought was not okay. The idea of gay thoughts never even crossed their minds, but they certainly crossed mine.

My best friend in church camp was a kid named Cody. Cody's family moved away when I was fifteen and I still don't know where they are. Cody and I knew each other for a few years before we were roommates in church camp. It was our last year, we were seventeen. I had the top bunk and Cody had the bottom. The room also housed three other bunk beds just like ours, occupied by other boys our age who kept us up at night with disgusting fart noises and the wild laughter that would follow. Cody and I had never talked much, but sometime during the symphony of armpit farts being emitted from the other boys, we formed a kinship as people who just wanted to go home.

Our last night at camp, there was a leak—one of those summer rain storms that keep the midwest from turning into a desert—and it caused water to start dripping through a crack in the cabin's ceiling. As the night wore on, the leak went from crack to hole to basically a full-on water faucet pouring directly onto my head. Eventually I got out of bed and made a pallet on the floor. I found a rusty old bucket under the sink in the bathroom and put it on the top bunk, which created the kind of soothing rain sound you hear on guided meditation CDs, and then attempted to sleep.

I tossed and turned on the cold, hard floor. It was wooden and smelled from the decades' worth of smelly teenage boy feet that had walked upon it every summer. Cody whispered to me through the pitch dark.

'*Pssst.* Hey. *Pssst.*' The sound came from seemingly nowhere.

'Hello?' I answered back to the darkness that sounded a lot like a boy my age.

'It's me. Bottom bunk. Cody.' Cody and I knew each other moderately well. We weren't best friends by any means, but we were familiar enough to know each other by voice and name. 'Why are you on the floor?'

I explained the leak and Cody offered to let me sleep in

his bed. It seemed to hold no hidden meanings, since I don't think either one of us even knew what hidden meanings were, so I quickly agreed, having long since realized I would be getting no sleep on the floor.

I crawled into Cody's twin bed that was so small and narrow we shared one pillow. It was the first time I'd slept in the same bed with another person since I was a toddler having nightmares. His breathing was heavy and strangely comforting and he smelled like the soap we always had in our kitchen at home. His sandy blond hair was still wet from a shower and his pillow was the slightest bit damp, but I didn't care, having just come from what was basically the worst water bed in history.

He didn't say good night and something told me he was still awake. I couldn't see him, but I could sense he wasn't asleep. He shifted, turning over on his side, and as he did, he grazed my back with, what I would eventually learn, was his erect penis. Without thinking about it, my penis was suddenly erect too. Now what?

After a moment or two, he turned over again and this time his penis seemed to be even more erect than the last time. Mine grew too, I could feel it in my Hanes, stretching out the waist band and the front pouch that holds your dick. I inched the slightest bit toward him and our penises touched. Through underwear and pyjamas, but still there they were—two hard cocks connecting, reaching out to each other in the dark. He didn't say a word, and I didn't either, but suddenly he was leading me into the bathroom.

I followed him in and there, in the pitch dark, we kissed. First quietly, sweetly, then progressively harder, more forceful, passionate, like I'd seen in the movies I watched without my parents knowing. He didn't touch my penis, and I didn't touch his. We just stood there, feeling each other with our hands, discovering each other's bodies and, for the first time, discovering what sex is. We eventually lay down on the cold hard tiles in the pitch black of a bathroom in a campground somewhere in the middle of Michigan, two boys, finally kissing.

We didn't speak of it the next day and that was the last time I ever saw him.

I wasn't scared by this occasion, far from it. I left with a sense of confidence, a final answer to a question that had been lingering at the back of my mind for as long as I could remember. Yes, I told myself, I *am* gay, but I didn't do a thing about it unless you count moving to Los Angeles a year later. Which, now that I think about it, is pretty gay. Even after three years in Los Angeles, I've still never done anything else. I don't know what I'm waiting for, maybe I'm scared. Either way, I'm getting tired of waiting.

Why, I wonder to myself, as I pull into the immaculate driveway of the Beverly Hills Hotel, am I thinking about Cody? Or that night? And the erect penises? And what does any of this have to do with my interviewing Taylor Grayson? And why, I wonder, looking down at my crotch, am I so hard right now?

CHAPTER 3

THE BEVERLY HILLS HOTEL is as grand on the inside as it appears on the outside. The closest I'd ever come to going inside was owning the DVD of *Troop Beverly Hills* starring Shelley Long and I'm pretty sure I loaned it out to my friend Melissa and never got it back.

The grounds are gorgeously lush, full of tall palm trees, flowers as bright and colourful as an American Apparel hoodie, and the kind of Hollywood glamour you can only find in movies. The whole place is abuzz with reporters, photographers, camera people and female publicists sporting severe blond bangs and the kind of power blazers Glenn Close wears on *Damages*. It's intimidating, especially since I have no idea what I'm doing and I'm attempting to cover an erection with my laptop bag.

I approach the check-in table. A no-nonsense woman in her mid-forties wearing obnoxiously hip cat-eye glasses asks, without looking up from her clipboard, 'Name?'

I give her my information and the name of Matty's editor. She sighs, as if I've asked her to make me a caramel macchiato with no whip, and checks me in. She then hands me my press credentials and tells me to wait in the ballroom to the left.

I make my way into the ballroom and, as I do, every single eye in the room looks at me. For a split second, I think about turning around to leave, but instead I find an empty seat next to some television reporter-type wearing way too much makeup and clothes that have been ironed within an inch of their lives. Looking around the room, I realize that I am, first of all, the youngest person there by at least a decade and a half, and second, that I'm the most underdressed of anyone. Everyone looks like they are auditioning to be the newest host of *American Idol*. These are professional reporters, the kind of people who prepared for this event in certain ways. Like seeing the movie ahead of time or not hiding a raging boner underneath their Macbooks. I try my best not to melt from intimidation, but it's hard not to. I spend a good fifteen minutes killing time on Taylor Grayson's Wikipedia page before a petite woman not much older than me walks over and asks, 'Are you from *The Star Report*?'

She startles me out of my Taylor Grayson haze and at first I just stare at her blankly before remembering that, yes, I *am* from *The Star Report*. She tells me to follow her and the rest of the group she's assembled up to the seventh floor. I follow behind a herd of blond reporters and guys with big fake smiles and tans the colour of Charlie Brown's pumpkin. We crowd into the elevator and I ride quietly as the reporters dish dirt on colleagues and celebrities. Someone asks someone about someone's surgery that someone's husband has recently performed and everyone in the elevator seems to know what they're talking about, or else everyone is really good at pretending they do.

The doors open to the seventh floor and we all file out into the hallway. I am told I'll be going in after the man in front of me, and I'm asked to stand 'on deck', ready to head in at a moment's notice. Something I've come to learn since moving to Hollywood is that no one takes Hollywood more seriously than Hollywood. The reporters, photographers and publicists scattered throughout the hotel hold the kind of high anxiety tension normally reserved for brain surgery. A large part of me wants to turn to the nervously fidgeting news anchor beside me and say, 'Hey. It's just a movie star.' But I don't because, well, I'm too nervous myself. I guess a little bit of Hollywood has begun to rub off on me.

Just then, the shiny oak door to the hotel room is opened by a very tall, menacing woman with jet black hair, a black power suit and a face that has undergone so much work she could pass for anything between thirty-five years old and a post-apocalyptic zombie. She points a long, skinny finger at me and I look around.

'Me?' I ask.

She rolls her eyes. 'Yes, you. Come in.'

She rushes me into the gorgeous hotel suite. Ornate furniture and artwork give the room a look of museum chic. Giant bright lights are set up around two chairs facing each other, with cameras positioned on either side. To the untrained eye, it could either be the set of a celebrity interview or an extremely formal police investigation.

The chairs are empty as she escorts me over and tells me to sit down. A microphone is immediately clipped inside my jacket and, without even asking, a man who smells like my seventh grade science teacher has his hand inside my shirt to hide the wire. It's all happening so fast that I don't even notice it when Taylor Grayson sits down.

I've never been to Europe. I have a passport, but the only place I've ever used it was Canada. And even then I was only there for twenty-four hours helping my cousin move into her dorm and I spent three of those hours helping her shop for groceries at a WalMart. I know a lot of people who have been to Europe, however, and they always come back in awe of the entire aura and look of the place. The gorgeous, epic buildings looking down on picturesque streets full of beautiful statues, people, cathedrals and landmarks. They always say the same thing: 'It took my breath away and I've never looked at the world the same way again.'

I have never experienced anything like that ... until now.

Taylor Grayson is flawless. Truly. Magazines don't do him justice, and neither do the movies he stars in. He has one of those faces, the kind of face it takes to garner fifteen million a movie, and the kind of pecs that deserve twenty. He's much bigger than I had expected, muscle-wise, of course—the closest thing to fat about Taylor Grayson is the heavy silver watch that glistens on his right wrist and probably cost more than what I paid in rent all of last year. His face is seemingly drawn on, the jaw line as if it has been chiseled to perfection by some great sculptor. And his chin. Oh! His chin! It sticks out just slightly, in the most perfect way, and there's a dimple, a really subtle, cute dimple right in the middle. Two other dimples frame his perfect smile, and when I say perfect smile, I mean *perfect* smile. I had no idea teeth could be that perfectly straight and white. They literally sparkle, like a Disney prince or a chewing gum commercial, and I am distracted for a moment trying to remember if Taylor Grayson has ever been the voice of a Disney prince or the face of a chewing gum ad. I go through the list of cartoon princes in my head and before I can make it past Aladdin he speaks.

'Hi, I'm Taylor. Pleasure to meet you.' He takes my hand and shakes it with a firm grip but not one of those 'I'm a man, dammit' kind of grips. A firm, confident grip, but not overwhelmingly so. It is, like pretty much everything else about Taylor Grayson, perfectly sexy. I turn my eyes to meet his and I audibly gulp but quickly attempt to cover for myself by coughing.

He's wearing a solid white v-neck t-shirt that fits him so well I can only assume it was custom made this very morning. He sports a pair of brown motorcycle boots, what you'd call 'ass kicking boots', and for a split second I imagine letting him do just that to me. A long silver necklace shines around his neck and dips into his shirt, then disappears into the small patch of hair that covers his chest. I can't help but wonder what is on the bottom of that necklace, and I'm lost in imagining sticking my hand down past that v, through the forest of chest hair and over the rock hard pectorals to find out.

'I'm uh ... Alex,' I manage to get out of my mouth, but I realize I must sound like someone who has never spoken out loud before and whose stutter is more obvious than the bulge in Taylor Grayson's jeans.

The woman who brought me in is getting annoyed I'm

slowing things down and she comes over to rush things along by asking, 'You're from where?'

Without thinking, I reply, 'Michigan.'

Taylor Grayson laughs, and it seems sincere. The publicist is not pleased, however, and grits her teeth while drilling me with her eyes. If Taylor is a Disney prince, this woman is Cruella DeVille without the puppies or cool car.

'What press outlet?'

I blush and am immediately even more frazzled. In a panic, I explain, 'I'm not normally a reporter for *The Star Report*. My friend, he's actually my roommate, is, but he's sick. Like really sick. Stomach style. It's bad. He asked me to fill in because he knows this is something I want to do. Write, that is. I've actually done a couple pieces for them in the past, well, one. I've never been on camera though, so just tell me when I should start and I will.'

The publicist stares at me blankly, and after a moment Taylor Grayson breaks the silence with another hearty laugh. Jesus Christ. Even his laughs are sexy.

'Can we begin?' the publicist asks, without phrasing it so much as a question but as a statement, as if to say, 'Now we will begin, dammit.'

I organize my notes into a neat stack in my lap, and at this point I've forgotten what I was going to ask to begin with. The camera operator gives me a five-second warning, Taylor Grayson straightens up in his chair, adjusts his t-shirt, smiles at me and whispers, 'You're going to be great.' Then he winks.

Crap. Why did he have to wink? I'm so flustered that I can barely even read the notes with everything I need to say sitting on my crotch, right on top of my cock—which, after that wink, is now, once again, completely hard.

'So ... uh ... Taylor. I mean, Mr Grayson—' I stutter.

'Taylor is fine,' he says with a grin.

'Why did you decide to do this movie?' It's the most I can come up with on the spot and I'm too nervous to try and read a note card. I can feel his publicist's eyes roll behind me. He goes on to explain that because this movie is about a firefighter he was really eager to do it.

'I grew up around a lot of firemen. My grandfather worked for the volunteer fire department in my hometown before I was born and my brother-in-law is part of the FDNY. These guys are risking their lives every day in situations that are unthinkable. That's why I'm donating half of my income from the movie to a charity that provides support for families who have lost a loved one in the line of duty.'

I'm speechless. Hot *and* nice? I really didn't know this existed in LA.

'Plus. I'm always looking for excuses to get greased up and shirtless. Aren't you?'

Taylor laughs that laugh again and my heart melts. I get lost in its deep sound for a moment but quickly try to come up with another question when the publicist gives me the sign to wrap it up. I've only asked one question and Matty is going to be pissed, but surely, I try telling myself, he'll understand.

'Thank you so much for meeting me today, Taylor. I can't wait to see *The Last Hero* in theatres starting this weekend! I'm Alex Kirby with *The Star Report*.'

The cameraman calls out 'Cut!' and the publicist rushes over to hurry me out. Taylor shakes my hand and looks deeply into my eyes, saying, 'Thank you. That was really fun.' He winks again and between the wink and the handshake I'm not sure I'm going to be able to make it down the hall.

What is it about this guy? I mean besides the obvious movie star looks, chiseled jaw line, Olympian body and air of pure, hot, hardcore sex, there's something else. A mystery. There's a story taking place behind his eyes and the more I look into them the more I'm dying to know just what that story is. Does he charm everyone this much or am I ... special? Before I can even consider this, the publicist is ushering me out the door.

As I pull the door open and walk into the chaos of the hallway, I glance back and there he is, Taylor Grayson, internationally beloved movie star, still smiling ... at me.

CHAPTER 4

I'M NOT SURE WHAT to tell Matty as I drive back down Sunset Boulevard toward home. I didn't screw up royally, but I certainly screwed up. One question. And not even a good question at that. 'Why did you choose this movie?' My five-year-old niece could have asked that.

They'll be messaging the tapes of the interview over to Matty's office within the hour, which means they'll likely watch them within the next two hours, which means they'll likely call Matty and complain that his friend made a complete moron of himself within the next four hours and, if my calculations are correct, by the time tonight rolls around I'll be the laughing stock of everyone who works for *The Star Report* and will possibly get Matty fired.

I arrive at our apartment with a giant jug of Gatorade to bribe Matty into not being mad at me. Matty always drinks Gatorade when he's sick or, more frequently, when he's hung over. I'd venture to guess that he spent a thousand dollars on Gatorade alone in the first year of our living together. Needless to say, Matty likes to have a good time, so I also picked up a bottle of vodka. Two birds. One stone.

When I walk into our living room, Matty is pacing the room on his phone, his shaggy red hair bounces back and forth as he goes. The TV is on mute and a woman with seemingly all gold teeth is sitting at a witness stand on one of those afternoon court shows. The text printed below her on the screen reads: 'Crystal. Made a terrible mistake.' I feel you, Crystal. I feel you.

'Uh huh. Okay. Well, I'll let him know. Alright, bye,' Matty says, hanging up the phone and looking at me strangely. I am bracing myself for the worst: I got Matty fired, the tapes are unusable, you can see my erection on camera, something.

'Sounds like you had an interesting afternoon,' Matty says with a sense of suspense.

'I can explain,' I say, dropping my bag onto the floor and beginning to make my case. 'I was nervous and when I got in there he—'Matty holds up his hand, in either a 'Stop what you're saying so I can chew you out' or a 'Stop in the name of love' kind of way. Here's to hoping it's the latter.

'He invited you to the premiere.'

'Who did?' I ask.

'Taylor Grayson,' he says simply, but in my mind it sounds more like 'Taaaaaaayyyyyyloooooorrr Grrrrrrraaaaaayyyyysoooooonnnnn' because time seems to slow down and the room seems to spin.

The only word I can get out of my mouth is, 'Huh?'

Matty sits his phone down and plops onto the couch. On TV, Crystal the muted defendant on the courtroom stand is now crying and the judge is *not* having it.

'His publicist called our offices and wanted to deliver the message that Taylor had more fun in your interview than he'd had all day. He liked that you didn't pretend to be something you weren't. What did you do in there?'

My mind is now spinning as I try to explain, 'I didn't do anything. That was the problem. I only asked him one question and it wasn't even a good question. I got so nervous. I've been around beautiful people before, but I've never been around Greek gods.'

Matty tells me to check my email, that the full invite and information are being forwarded to my address. There are so many questions going through my head in this moment, the first of which is that I need him to be sure this wasn't a mistake. I want to know which publicist called. An assistant? An assistant to an assistant? Or that woman with the jet black hair and the face that looked like one of Tim Burton's early sketches for *The Nightmare Before Christmas*?

'The premiere is tomorrow night. At the Arclight in Hollywood followed by a big party by the pool at the Hollywood Roosevelt Hotel. The invitation is for you and a guest. And there's one other thing. A pretty big thing.'

A *big* thing? As big as Taylor Grayson's bulge which I can't seem to stop thinking about? As big as the triceps bursting out of his white t-shirt? As big as the orgasm I always have when jerking off to his shower scene in *Yard*?

'Taylor personally requested that you do his first post-premiere interview, which will run as an exclusive for *The Star Report*. He's going to sit down with you right after the movie screening!'

'He *what*?' I shout out, a lot louder than necessary, but I simply cannot contain myself. Sure, this will be great for my career, but more importantly, why me? Why did he enjoy our interview so much? It couldn't be as black and white as my not being phony. There are tons of not-phony reporters in Los Angeles. Okay, maybe not, but still, why me?

'So you'll do it?' Matty asks with no sense of irony, which causes me to burst into laughter for the first time all day.

'Of course. Of course I'll do it,' I say, out of breath.

'Good. I'll let my boss know. I *cannot* believe this!' Matty bounces into the kitchen and pours some of the Gatorade into a glass. 'P.S., I'm obviously your plus-one.'

Moments later, Matty calls the office to confirm that I'll be there, and I lie down on the sofa to catch my breath, process my thoughts, daydream about Taylor's perfectly flat stomach and his happy trail that guides one down its path to where? The promised land? I glance at the TV, and Crystal has happily won her case. She's rejoicing in her seat. Again, I think, I feel you, girl.

CHAPTER 5

AS SOMEONE WHO HAS never been to a Hollywood premiere before, I can confidently vouch that the premiere of *The Last Hero* is the best premiere I've ever been to. I've been to a handful of other swanky Hollywood functions, but always as a waiter, and even then the fanciest one was at Kirstie Alley's house. It was nice, but it smelled like dog hair and the only other famous person there was the guy who used to sell those electronic grills on infomercials.

A giant red carpet snakes its way around the Arclight Cinedome, a mob of reporters and photographers makes up the mosh pit of cameras on the other side. People driving by slow down, honk and shout, 'Taylor, I love you!' What a mind trip that must be, to have so many strangers screaming your name.

Our tickets permit us to walk the red carpet and I'm more than a little nervous. I'm first struck by just how red the red carpet really is. They're not lying when they call it that. This thing is so red it looks like it was made from the fur of Elmo's parents, or blood. Or both.

'I'll lead the way,' Matty declares, straightening his green skinny tie and flipping his Bieber bangs out of his face. Matty fancies himself a Hollywood socialite and I suppose you could argue that he's right. He's been to countless premieres and parties and once Blake Lively recognized him in Best Buy. I normally find Matty's Hollywood power player act a bit tiresome, but tonight I welcome it with open arms.

Matty leads us down the carpet, stopping to smile for cameras as if they want his picture.

'What are you doing?' I whisper to him as he does his best Kardashian stance.

'If you act like a famous person in Hollywood, people will just assume you *are* a famous person. Pose!' he instructs me through a tight smile.

I roll my eyes but try it anyway. When in Rome.

A handful of clueless photographers snap our picture. Matty is right: everyone in Hollywood is as stupid as he says. Speaking of stupid, Melanie Griffith appears and all eyes move to her. Matty is annoyed, but I think it's an honour to be upstaged by Melanie Griffith.

'Let's get inside,' Matty says, yanking me along. 'Now that Melanie and Antonio are here, we might as well be lesbians at the Country Music Awards.'

Inside, everyone is decked in black tie and fancy gowns and, like everywhere else in Hollywood, everyone is pretending to know each other. I don't do well in crowds like this, I get nervous and insecure and would pretty much always rather be at home watching *House Hunters International*. Just then, a finger taps me on the back. I turn and spot Taylor's publicist from the Beverly Hills Hotel interview.

'Alex, yes?' she asks, looking me up and down. I wonder to myself if she's going to notice that I'm wearing black shoes with a brown belt.

'Hi. Thanks for the invitation. I'm *so* excited to be here.'

She rolls her eyes. 'I'm Belinda Chase, Taylor's publicist. Follow me.'

Belinda speaks with such authority that I don't even think twice, I just follow her. I would follow her to my seat, to the concession stand, to wherever they get the water in Fiji bottles ... which now that I think about it is probably Fiji.

Matty and I are quietly following her when she stops and stares Matty down.

'Who are you?' she asks, her words as sharp as the heels of her Jimmy Choos.

'I'm Matty Hansen. I work for *The Star Report*. Alex was actually filling in for me when he interviewed Taylor. I'm his plus-one.'

Without a second thought, Belinda smiles, nods and instructs Matty to find his seat and says that I'll join him in a moment. Matty attempts to respond, but before he can even get one word out, Belinda has whisked me through a door and down an empty hallway.

Part of me gets a little thrill out of being the one to receive special treatment. Matty always gets to do cool stuff, but tonight is my turn. I'm going to do a sit-down exclusive interview with Taylor Grayson at my very first Hollywood premiere. Screw *Oprah's New Chapter*, it's time for my first.

Before I can ask Belinda where we're going, we arrive at a door with a sign that reads: 'Please knock.' She doesn't. We walk into the room, which is a small conference-room-style space with a catered spread of finger foods, a fully stocked bar and Taylor Grayson, sitting on a sofa reading on his iPad. He looks up and— I'm not joking—his teeth actually sparkle.

'You came,' Taylor says with a grin.

'Well. Yeah,' I say, stopping myself from adding 'duh' in an effort to look not quite so lame.

'I'll be back in five. I've got to do some damage control with Nancy O' Dell.' Belinda says, leaving Taylor and me alone. For a moment, it's strangely quiet.

'Hungry?' Taylor asks, motioning to the table full of food.

'I'm actually okay. I ate before. That is a lot of food,' I say, eyeing a literal tower of egg rolls.

'I know. They always do this kind of crap. Who has ever wanted to eat that many sliders before watching themselves in a movie?' Taylor says, getting up from the sofa and straightening his tie in front of the mirror. He looks even more perfect standing up and I wonder for a moment if he somehow got even taller.

'So, are we doing the interview now?' I ask, looking around the room for a camera.

Taylor looks at me, confused. Then, after a moment, he replies, 'Oh, no. Not until later. After the movie.'

I nod, but inside I'm beyond flustered trying to figure out what the hell I'm doing here.

'What do you do for fun?' Taylor asks, looking down at his humongous watch.

I'm taken aback by the question, mainly because it is the last thing I expected him to ask, second only to 'Why is Faye Resnick famous?', and also because I'm not really sure what I do for fun.

'I watch a lot of TV.' I say, then immediately wish I hadn't said that.

'Ha. Well, what do you do that isn't watching TV?'

I have to think about this for a moment. What have I recently done for fun? Well, yesterday it was jerk off and fantasize about Taylor Grayson, but that's probably not the response he's looking for.

'I love vinyl. Like records. I got a record player a few months ago and now I'm, like, obsessed with going to yard sales and looking for music,' I tell him. It's true and the only 'hobby' I can think of.

'What's your favorite record?' he asks, untying and retying his crooked tie.

I'm taken aback again by the casual questioning. I had not expected to be talking about records tonight. I have to think about it because I don't want to say something ridiculous like 'Bette Midler's *Divine Madness*.' While I may or may not have played that record so many times I've worn it out, I can't imagine a more ridiculously gay thing to say, but then again, why do I even care what he thinks to begin with?

'I just got a James Taylor album this past weekend that's basically all I've been listening to. It's perfect. I love that era. I've also got Simon and Garfunkel. Some of them are hard to come by. Like Joni Mitchell's *Blue*.'

He nods. 'Joni is great,' he says with a smile, looking at me, seeming to take all of me in with his eyes. His smile turns to a grin, a mysterious grin that has a not-so-hidden motive, but one I can't quite figure out. I've started to sweat and I'm wondering if I remembered to wear deodorant. Please, God. Let me, just this once, have remembered to wear deodorant.

Belinda knocks on the door and Taylor tells her to come in.

'It's time for you on the carpet. You ready?' she asks, poking her head in.

'Sure. Give me one more minute.' Taylor says, closing the door and turning to me.

'I wanted to see you again. There's something about you ... something I can't quite put my finger on, but it's something I like.'

I turn redder than the carpet that Melanie Griffith was just posing on outside.

'I have a proposition for you, but it'll have to wait until later. Are you open to hearing about it?' he asks, very seriously—so seriously that for a split second I feel like I'm in an episode of *The Sopranos*. I've gotten lost in thinking about how much I like Edie Falco when he snaps me back to reality. 'Well?' he asks.

'Yes. Yes, I'm open to hearing about it. Very,' I add, more confused than I've ever been before. Taylor Grayson might just be one of the most serious people I've ever met. Even when he smiles or cracks a joke, there's still something so very serious about him. It could come across as arrogance if I weren't too busy undressing him with my eyes.

'Good,' he says with that mysterious grin again. 'I think it's something we'll both enjoy.'

He opens the door and walks into the hallway. I stand

back, wondering why Taylor Grayson spent five minutes before his premiere talking to me about vinyl collecting. He keeps walking down the hall and, somewhere along the way, he makes the transformation from mysterious hot guy talking to my weirdo ass about Joni Mitchell to internationally beloved movie star. He opens the door to head outside and I hear what must be hundreds, maybe even thousands, of people scream his name in unison:

'Taylor!' they cheer, and I feel like cheering right along with them.

CHAPTER 6

AS I SIT IN the darkened theater, I have absolutely no idea what is happening in *The Last Hero*. From the reaction of people around me, it's very good, but I gave up trying to focus twenty minutes in. My mind is focused on one thing and one thing only. This alleged proposition from Taylor Grayson.

I haven't told Matty about it because right as I got to my seat the movie started, and I was not about to whisper during a movie with Melanie Griffith sitting one row in front of me. Matty seems into the movie, everybody does, and Taylor looks incredible. He's in his firefighter uniform for the majority of the movie, and when he's not, he's either sweaty and shirtless or sweaty and wearing a tank top. I may not be paying much attention to the movie, but if there's one thing I can say about it, it's that Taylor Grayson is sweaty for the majority of *The Last Hero*—and that's quite alright with me! His sweat is the most gorgeous sweat I've ever seen, the way it clings to his chest hair and drips down the crease between his two pecs and onto his greased-up stomach.

The movie feels endless. It seems like hours ago that Taylor and I were standing in his dressing room, but when I check my watch, I realize it's only been forty-five minutes. I attempt to follow the story in an effort to make time pass quicker, but it doesn't work. Time continues to slide by at a snail's pace and Taylor seems to be wearing a shirt less and less.

Matty leans over to me and whispers, 'He might just be the world's most perfect man.'

I nod, and I've never agreed with something more in my life. 'I'd pay a billion dollars to make him gay just for one day.'

When the credits *finally* roll, after a very teary scene between Taylor and his drug addict mother, played by the aforementioned Melanie Griffith, I turn to Matty. But before we can start talking about the movie, Belinda taps me on the shoulder from behind my seat.

I turn and she once more instructs us to follow her.

We go down that same hall from earlier and back into that same conference room. The food has been cleared away but the bar is still there. Two cameras and some lights have been set up facing the chairs in the corner.

A sound engineer comes over to me and sticks a lapel microphone through my shirt and clips it to my collar, just like the other day at the hotel.

'Test that for me,' he tells me just as Taylor walks into the room, causing me to come up speechless. 'Hello? Test that for me?' the soundman says, getting annoyed.

'Say something, Alex,' Matty adds.

'Oh, sorry. Test. Test. One, two, three. Test,' I blurt out, not taking my eyes off Taylor.

As Taylor takes a seat, they put his microphone on him. To do so, he unbuttons four buttons of his shirt, revealing his happy trail and a great set of those muscles that really insanely in-shape people have around their stomach and hips. The ones that form a V going down to one's crotch. I don't know what they're called because I've never had them. I imagine what it would feel like to follow those muscles down to his crotch using just my tongue.

'Okay. Let's get going. We need him at the party in twenty minutes,' Belinda says, rushing everyone into place. Matty smiles at me from across the room and gives me a thumb's up. He's either letting me know that I'm doing a good job or he's acting out what I'm imagining Taylor Grayson doing to my butt.

I learnt my lesson last time. I've come prepared with notes and questions. I straighten up in the very comfortable chair just as the camera's red light begins flashing.

'Hello, this is Alex Kirby with *The Star Report*. I'm here with the one and only Taylor Grayson, literally moments after the premiere of his new movie *The Last Hero*, getting *The Star Report*'s exclusive first interview with Mr Grayson after seeing his new film. Thank you so much for sitting down with me,' I say, doing my best Ryan Seacrest.

Taylor smiles at me, he seems impressed by my 'go get 'em' attitude.

'First of all, call me Taylor. Mr Grayson is my grandfather,' he jokes.

I go on. My questions are general celebrity interview questions and Taylor answers them with general celebrity interview answers. He's charming, lovable, sexy, smart and perfectly 'on'. The interview is total fluff and I still don't understand why he wanted me, of all people, to conduct it.

We wrap up the interview and I thank Taylor for his time.

'The pleasure was all mine,' he says and winks at me again. How many winks are we at, at this point? Ten? I've stopped counting.

The cameraman calls cut, and the sound engineer has his hands up my shirt taking back his microphone. Belinda looks down at her BlackBerry and calls out, 'Shit. I've got to get over to the party. *Vanity Fair* is seated with *Vogue* and somebody is bound to cut somebody with a salad fork if I don't intervene.'

She quickly forces the cameraman, the sound guy, the team of couture-wearing assistants and even Matty out the door and calls back to Taylor: 'You've got a car out front waiting for you. I'll see you there.' She points at a young assistant, a girl who will most likely grow up to have as many face lifts as Belinda someday. 'Charlotte, will you see to it that Taylor gets to his car?'

The assistant nods and follows Belinda out into the hall. Once again, it's just Taylor and me standing alone in the room. I wonder for a moment where Matty ended up but can't manage to actually care.

'Well, I don't know about you but there's no way I'm going to that party without getting at least a little drunk first,' Taylor says, removing his suit jacket. His crisp white dress shirt is extremely tight around his enormous biceps, and from where I'm standing I can smell his musky cologne.

'Want to get a drink?' he asks with that now familiar grin.

I turn, looking back at the fully stocked bar and say, 'Sure.'

'Oh, not here. I'm dying to go somewhere. Let's take the car and we can stop by my favorite spot before the party.' He heads for the door. 'Do you have your car here?'

I confess that I don't have a car. 'I took the bus.'

Taylor makes a face as if I've just told him I drive a Mary Kay pink Cadillac. 'There's a bus in LA?'

We begin making our way down the hall as I ask him, 'Didn't your publicist say you had to be at the party in ten minutes?' It suddenly occurs to me that I would follow this guy anywhere. You know that saying your parents always had: 'If all your friends were doing it, would you do it too?' With Taylor Grayson, it actually applies. I'm fairly certain I'd do anything and everything he asked.

'As you'll come to find out, Alex, publicists' jobs are to tell me what to do ... and my job is to pretend to listen to them. And lucky for me, I'm really good at pretending.'

He winks—we're now at eleven times I guess—and we step into the town car waiting in the alley outside.

CHAPTER 7

MATTY TEXTS ME WHILE Taylor and I are riding in the town car through the back streets of Hollywood: 'Where r u??????'

Taylor glances over at my phone. 'Uh oh. Is your friend upset?'

I blush, realizing he can see my phone. 'I didn't tell him I wasn't going to the party. He's my plus-one, so he probably thinks I ditched him—'

Taylor interrupts me. 'Well, I can drop you off there now if you'd rather.'

'NO!' I say, a little too quickly and a little too loudly. 'No. It's fine. I'm just going to let him know I'll be there late.'

We pull up to what appears to be an old storefront on Hollywood Boulevard. It appears abandoned, with a metal garage door covered in graffiti pulled down over the windows. The driver opens the door for us, Taylor hops out and I follow. Before I can even ask where we are, Taylor knocks on a brown metal door, which immediately opens.

I'm beginning to wonder if I'm going to be a part of my first hardcore drug deal.

We go in and, after turning a corner, find ourselves in an elegant, dimly-lit bar with enormous light fixtures made out of deer antlers hanging from the ceiling. The walls are windowless and painted a dark shade of brown. Dark green leather booths line the walls and a giant mahogany bar sits in the centre of the room. The bar is nearly empty, with two people in one of the booths and two others on stools. They're smoking at their tables. It's like we've stepped into an episode of *Mad Men*. A hipster bartender with a haircut so hip it's almost normal waves hello to Taylor as he approaches the bar.

'The usual?' The hipster bartender asks, putting two empty wine glasses in front of him. Taylor nods and leads me to a booth in the back. As we go, I notice that no one turns and stares at Taylor the way people have done everywhere else I've seen him. In fact, the people in this bar seem unsurprised to see Taylor and look far more curious as to who I might be.

'Where are we?' I ask, trying to seem cool and unimpressed but secretly thinking, 'Holy shit! Is this a speakeasy?'

Taylor explains that this is a private members-only bar and that only a handful of people know about it. He explains that it's a popular spot for people who enjoy a little privacy. Hollywood code for celebrity hangout.

The bartender brings over two glasses of wine and walks away. Taylor looks over at me with his usual serious expression. 'So, tell me, Alex Kirby. What do you want to be when you grow up?'

'You remember my last name,' I say, honestly shocked that he even remembers my first.

'I have a very good memory. So?' he asks, bringing me back to his original question.

'Well, I want to write. Journalism kind of stuff.' He stares into me, his crystal blue eyes somehow getting bluer. 'That's why I moved out here. I love writing about movies but it's a hard bracket to get into. I guess acting is the same way, right?'

'Not really. Or at least not when you look like me,' he says with a completely straight face. I'm taken aback, but before I can say anything else he adds, 'Kidding. Of course it's hard. Lucky for me, I come from stupidly rich parents and happen to have extremely good luck.'

I wonder for a moment, just how rich Taylor Grayson is. 'Good luck, huh?'

'Certainly. No matter what it is, I always find a way to get exactly what I want,' he says, putting his hands behind his head and stretching out his back. If he weren't so damn hot, I'd think he was a disgusting egomaniac.

'Well, cheers to good luck,' I declare, holding up my glass of wine.

He raises his and adds: 'No. To getting exactly what we want.' He smiles and I wonder for a moment if Taylor Grayson might know exactly what I want, but quickly remember that there's no possible way he could.

My phone lights up again. It's Matty and I read his text.

'What does your friend say?' Taylor asks.

'He's at the party. He asked if I'm with you,' I tell him.

'Is he your boyfriend?'

'Matty? No. Not at all. He's my roommate. Just that. He's more like a brother. Or a sister,' I tell him, which is true. Matty and I have about as much sexual chemistry as I have with my seventy-eight-year-old landlady, Charlene.

'Well, that's very good to know.' He grins, finishing his wine in one gulp, then stands up. 'I've got to get to that party before Belinda calls the National Guard. Thank you for joining me. I really enjoyed this.'

I stand up and I want to hug him, to wrap my arms around his firm tree trunk of a body. I want to bury myself in his shoulder and lose myself in his smell. But instead we shake hands, like we've just had a business meeting, and he goes with no mention of the 'proposition'.

I watch him walk to the door, his walk is more of a slow, confident stride. Who knew a walk could be so sexual? I'm watching the way his perfect butt sways from side to side, just so—and it isn't until he's out the door that I remember he's my ride, and that I've just been stranded by one of the sexiest men alive at a celebrities-only speakeasy somewhere in the middle of Hollywood. Was it something I said?

CHAPTER 8

I'M IN MY GYM shorts and cut-off Miranda Lambert T-shirt by the time Matty gets home. I texted him an hour or so ago letting him know I wouldn't be coming to the party. I lied and told him I wasn't feeling well. Which wasn't that big a lie; I really wasn't feeling very well, but it was only because of how things ended with Taylor. He didn't even invite me to come with him when he left the bar—he literally stranded me on Hollywood Boulevard. What the hell had all of that been about? Was his proposition just to have a drink with me then disappear? Or was I less interesting than he'd hoped?

Matty walks in the front door, slightly tipsy.

'Well, look who it is. Mr Mystery Man,' Matty slurs, leaning against the sofa to stand up.

'Matty, I'm so sorry.'

'What the hell happened? One minute we're at the movie and the next you're being taken away by some woman who looks like the mother-in-law on *The Real Housewives of Miami*.'

I could tell Matty wasn't all that upset, mostly just eager for a story—and a story I was about to give him.

'You aren't going to believe this, but I was with Taylor Grayson,' I say. The first time I've got to say it out loud. I impressed even myself. 'And he took me to some secret celebrity speakeasy to have a drink before he went to the party. But then—'

Matty interrupts me. 'A speakeasy? Jesus Christ. Why can't hipsters just leave the world as it is?' Matty says, making a really solid point. 'So why didn't you come to the party?'

This is the part of the story that would sound the least glamorous when coming out of my mouth and I was dreading having to say it: 'Well, we were joking, having a good time, and he asked if we were boyfriends—'

'You and I?' Matty says, a little too shocked if you ask me.

'Yeah. And I said no and then he said good to know and left.' I finish the story and stare at him blankly, hoping for some words of wisdom. 'I'm worried he got freaked out ... maybe because I'm gay. Or more likely because I'm lame.'

Matty bursts into laughter, which continues for a few moments. 'Do you honestly think he just *now* realized you're gay, Alex?'

Matty is probably right, I'm not the straightest arrow in the world, but it's not like I'm *that* flamboyant. There are probably tons of people who wouldn't guess I'm gay. Sure, those people would have to be blind and deaf, but that's neither here nor there.

'I felt like we were becoming friends, but then he literally disappeared.'

Matty stares at me and shakes his head.

'I can't believe I'm about to say what I'm about to say.'

I honestly have no idea what he is about to say.

'Has it occurred to you that maybe Taylor Grayson wants to get in your pants?'

I get an immediate erection and my left armpit starts sweating. No, that has not occurred to me because I'm not delusional. Everybody knows that Taylor Grayson is the world's biggest playboy, and everybody knows he could have any woman he wants, or man for that matter—but he wouldn't because he's straight.

'He's had some of the most famous girlfriends in the world, Matty.'

'And some of the most famous break-ups, too,' he adds. 'I've got to go to bed because ... well ... I'm drunk and if I don't, I'm going to pass out on the floor into the nachos I will inevitably order. But think about it, Alex, maybe there's more to Taylor Grayson than meets the eye. Maybe he wants to learn more about you before he makes a move.'

He stumbles into his bedroom and closes the door. A second later, I hear his body hit the bed. It's suddenly very quiet in our apartment and I sit wondering: does Matty have a point? And if so, will I ever see Taylor Grayson again?

CHAPTER 9

THAT NIGHT I HAVE a dream. I'm at the bar Taylor took me to, but instead of leaving I go into the bathroom and forget to lock the door. It's a single-person restroom with a toilet and urinal. I've just finished peeing and am washing my hands when the door opens.

I let out an obligatory 'Someone's in here!' before turning to see Taylor standing in the doorway. He's grinning that grin again, but this time it isn't so mysterious. This time, in the world of the dream at least, I know what he wants—and what he wants is me.

He steps inside and closes the door behind him. He remembers to lock it. I'm nervous but not confused. I know what's going to happen and I'm ready. I'm confident in a way I've never been before. I feel sexy and desired and Taylor looks, as usual, beyond hot.

He comes towards me, gets extremely close up to my face—so close we're almost kissing but not quite. His breath is hot on my face as he tells me to get on the floor. He speaks so authoritatively that I do exactly as I'm told. 'On your knees,' he commands, like a drill sergeant in a homoerotic war movie from the fifties. I obey.

He unzips his fly and grabs me by the chin, tilting my head as far back as it can go, so far back it feels like I'm getting my hair washed in one of those weird hair washing sinks they have at salons.

'How much do you want it?'

I'm speechless, but nod eagerly, excited, desperate. I don't know how much I want it, I just know I want it. And I'm not even a hundred per cent sure what the 'it' in question is. Though I have a pretty good idea.

'No. I want to hear you tell me how much you want it. How much you need it.'

I can tell from the growing bulge in his pants that his cock is getting harder and harder by the minute and I want nothing more than to pull it out. Nervously, I reach my hand forward, and his eyes on me are maddening—still that gorgeous baby blue, but now wider with a sense of fury and immediacy.

'I want you to suck my cock,' he tells me. 'Do you want to do that?'

I nod. I've never wanted anything as much in my life.

'Say yes sir!'

I say it.

'Louder.'

I say it louder.

'Louder!'

This time I scream it at the top of my lungs, so loud that people in the Glendale Galleria Mall could probably hear it.

And that's when I wake up—panting, covered in sweat, and having just had my first wet dream since I was sixteen.

CHAPTER 10

WHEN I WAKE UP IN the morning, I'm feeling pretty groggy, likely because of the drinks at the premiere and the not-so-successful date with Taylor afterward. I don't drink very often, or rather I don't drink very often for a gay guy in his twenties, the standard for which is that of Buster Keaton in the years before his liver gave out entirely. I feel disappointed when I remember the dream the night before, not because it wasn't a great dream—and it was a *really* great dream—but because I remember that Taylor hadn't come into the bathroom at the bar, that he'd actually just left me there.

Today I'm doing what a lot of successful people in Los Angeles call 'paying your dues'. Which to those of us who are the due-payers is code for: cater-waitering. I hate being a cater-waiter. The last time I did it, I spent literally four hours wandering around a car showroom repeating the same phrase over and over: 'Tuna tartar? Tuna tartar?' After a while, I got tired and started mumbling and by the end of the night it sounded more like 'Luna Lamar,' which I'm pretty sure was the name of a drag queen I met in Dayton, Ohio.

In the living room, I'm surprised to find Matty doing just that: living. He's on the couch with a big bowl of cereal watching *The Today Show*.

'You had quite the night last night, huh?'

I have absolutely no idea what he's talking about. Does he not remember our entire conversation when he got home and I explained how Taylor left me at the bar? Surely he's not going to make me relive that story. Again.

'Whom did you have over?' he asks with the enthusiasm of a fifteen-year-old girl or a middle-aged pervert awaiting a One Direction concert. Again, I'm super confused.

'I heard you ... you were ... well, loud. So who was it? Spill.'

I suddenly realize what he heard, and it wasn't me getting laid. It was me dreaming about getting laid. By Taylor Grayson no less. Matty heard me having a sex dream and now he thinks I've finally lost my virginity. I have two choices here: I can either tell him the sad truth, which makes me look about as desperate as the homeless woman who looks sort of like my fifth grade teacher but with an eyepatch and who stands outside the Jamba Juice near our apartment. Or I can play dumb and pretend I have no idea what he's talking about.

'I have no idea what you're talking about. I had some nightmares. Maybe that's what you heard?' I say, going into the kitchen to pour some coffee and pull the plug on this conversation entirely.

When I enter the kitchen, there's a strange package sitting on our table.

'What's this?' I call out.

'Oh. That came for you this morning. From some messenger service,' Matty says.

I stare at the package. There's no return address. It's a large box, but when I shake it, I can tell there's something smaller inside. I think the last time I got a box sent to me was when my grandmother made me a lap quilt for my eighteenth birthday. From shaking the box, I can tell this is not a lap quilt. For a split second, the thought that this is a bomb sent by a terrorist does enter my mind, but before I can rationalize calling the FBI, I decide to open it.

Inside, there's an absurd amount of bubble wrap. I suspect that someone simply sent me an entire box of bubble wrap, which wouldn't be the worst gift I've ever received (being a guy who has opened two separate birthday gifts from two separate people on two separate occasions to find a copy of Alicia Silverstone's vegan cookbook).

I begin unwrapping the layers upon layers of bubble wrap and finally get to ... a record.

Holy shit. It's Joni Mitchell. *Blue.* The record I told Taylor Grayson about last night. The record I said I didn't have. My heart skips a beat and I reach inside the box and find a note. I take a deep breath just so I can put off reading it for one more second. I want this anticipation to last a lifetime.

The card reads, simply: 'For your collection. TG. 310-343-1124.'

'So what is it?' Matty says, appearing in the doorway.

I drop the note into the box. 'It's a record.'

Matty walks in and picks up the album, inspecting it. 'Who sent you a record?' he asks skeptically.

I don't want to tell Matty anything. He is a professional big mouth—by which I mean a reporter. All he'd have to do is tweet this to one of his thousands of followers and Taylor would never speak to me ever again.

'Just a friend who—' before I can finish, Matty's hand has already pulled the note from the box.

'Holy. Shit. TG? This is from Taylor Grayson, isn't it?'

Too late. And frankly too early in the morning to try and come up with a believable story, so I just come clean and tell him the truth: yes it is from Taylor Grayson, no I don't know why he sent it and no I don't plan on keeping it.

'Why the hell wouldn't you keep it? It's from a movie star. Isn't there some sort of unspoken Los Angeles rule about keeping anything a celebrity gives you?' Matty says, flipping the record over and reading the back. For a moment I wonder to myself whether Matty is being sarcastic or not. Which speaks volumes for how much I know about how Hollywood works.

'This is a really rare record. It's worth a lot of money and it's never been opened. I can't just keep it. It's too nice,' I tell him. But in the back of my head I'm wondering if maybe I should keep it. I mean, it is a gift after all.

'And it's autographed!' Matty says, showing me a note written on the back. I grab the record. He's right, and not only is it autographed but Joni Mitchell herself has written a personal note. To me!

Dear Alex,

I hear this is one of your favourites. I'm honoured to be part of your collection and hope you'll enjoy these songs as much as I enjoyed writing them.

With love, Joni

Joni! She called herself Joni. Like we're old friends from the beauty shop: 'Oh hey, Joni, how are the kids?' How the hell did Taylor Grayson find an unopened *Blue* album, track down Joni Mitchell and get her to sign it all before 10 a.m.? Doesn't Joni Mitchell live on a weed farm outside San Francisco or something? I've never pictured her in any other situation.

Matty grabs my hand and stares me in the eye.

'He gave you his number too. Do you know what this means?' Matty says, the most serious he's sounded since he made the decision to buy a pair of men's Uggs. 'It means he likes you. Like, *really* likes you.'

I feel my face redden.

'I can't believe this. Taylor Grayson is ga—'

Before he can finish his sentence, I put my finger over his lips. 'Don't. Don't say anything. This cannot leave this kitchen,' I insist.

'But the record player is in the living room,' he says, poking me in the stomach. 'I cannot believe my roommate is going to be Taylor Grayson's boyfriend!'

'Neither of us knows why he gave me the record,' I tell him. 'And neither of us should be talking about this to anyone. Ever. Understand?' I look at Matty the way

I always look at him when I'm trying to make a serious point. It's a combination of brooding, seriousness and the way Whoopi Goldberg looks at Barbara Walters when she says something stupid on *The View*. I grab the note from his hand and stick it in my pocket for safekeeping. 'If this ends up on *The Star Report* or Twitter or *anywhere*, I will literally kill you,' I say with a commanding, powerful tone. That's when I remember I'm late for my cater-waiter gig, and all powerful or commanding fantasies vanish as I rush off to serve a bunch strangers tuna tartar.

* * *

Cater-waitering is the kind of job that leaves your mind to wander. There's only so many times you can ask someone if they'd like another slider before one's mind begins to make grocery lists and fantasy-cast a movie about *The Real Housewives of Beverly Hills*. Laura Dern as Kim Richards, by the way. Today, however, my thoughts are fixed on one thing. Taylor Grayson.

His note is burning a hole in my pocket. I can't seem to stop thinking about it. Should I call him? I can't. What would I say? I mean, besides 'Thank you for the record but I can't possibly accept it ... Oh, p.s. are you secretly gay? Oh, and p.p.s. I had a wet dream about you. How do you know Joni Mitchell?'

But what if Matty is right? What if Taylor Grayson does 'like-like' me? That thought lasts a good five seconds before I snap back to reality. No. That's impossible. He's just extremely polite, efficient and sexy. So *very* sexy. My mind wanders to the way his hair swoops across his forehead so perfectly. The way his pants hug his hips and crotch. The way his lips pucker just slightly, like two soft memory foam pillows.

I continuously try to change my thoughts: I think of laundry, I think of Laura Dern as Kim Richards, I think of what I need to pick up from the grocery store on the way home, I'm out of soap ... remember to buy soap. But every thought somehow leads me back to Taylor. Soap, I imagine him in the shower ... his tan, muscled body covered in white soap suds and the smooth way it would feel to the touch. The way it would feel to rub the soap into his wet, hot skin.

'Hey, are you okay?' Josh startles me back to reality. 'You've been staring off into space for, like, five minutes.'

Josh is a friend I've met through countless cater-waitering gigs together. Josh is a struggling actor, and one that I suspect will be very successful someday. He's got a very handsome face, really pretty, long blond hair, and, judging solely by the one time Matty and I saw him do a production of *Proof* at a theatre in Santa Monica, he's a great actor. He's also endlessly sweet, the type of guy who brings you soup if you say you're sick on Facebook.

Josh is one the few guys I've met that, if I didn't have a hundred pounds worth of emotional baggage, I could probably date. He's certainly a catch, but I'm just not sure he's what I'm fishing for.

'Yeah. I'm fine. I've just ... I've got a lot on my mind,' I tell him, which isn't a lie.

'I'm sorry. Like what?'

'Oh, just work stuff,' I tell him, which *is* a lie.

'Tell you what, some friends and I are going to get drinks after we leave here. You should come. Blow off some steam.'

I'm not a much for parties or bars or anywhere that is loud and crowded. I much prefer the comforts of my sofa and a pint of frozen yogurt to a loud club and a vodka tonic. Matty goes out three or four nights a week, but partying just isn't my cup of tea. Or rather, I'd prefer staying home and having an actual cup of tea.

'Come on. You never come out. I insist. It'll help you clear your mind,' Josh tells me, flicking a long strand of blond hair behind his ear.

Maybe he's right, maybe that's exactly what I need, a night to drink off all these confusing feelings about Taylor Grayson, the mystery man.

I could probably lose my virginity to Josh if I really wanted to. I'm sure it would even be fun, but I guess I just want my first time to be something more than that. My mind for a moment moves to thinking about losing said virginity to Taylor, but I quickly snap out of it, just in time to refill a woman's mimosa.

Once the day finally ends and we've finished cleaning up, I text Matty to invite him to join us. He, of course, agrees. I ride with Josh over to West Hollywood, which is the gayest of the gay here in Los Angeles. This is where shirtless go-go boys smoking cigarettes with drag queens are more common than Starbucks.

You can practically smell the gayness as your car pulls past La Cienaga Boulevard and down through Santa Monica

Boulevard and its countless gay bars, sex shops and very expensive male clothing stores where the mannequins in the windows have better abs than I do.

I almost never go to West Hollywood. It's how I feel about Katie Couric's talk show: I'm glad it's there, but that doesn't mean I want to make it a part of my daily life. Going out in West Hollywood is best left for special occasions, like the anniversary of the day you moved to Los Angeles or when you're trying to get your mind off one of the world's biggest movies stars who may or may not want in your pants.

When my mother came to visit me a few years ago, Matty and I took her out in 'WeHo'. That's the slang term for West Hollywood because honestly, who has the time to say all those words? Somewhere between the six-foot-five Dolly Parton impersonator and the herd of shirtless boys clearly headed off to a nearby orgy, Mom's head almost exploded. I still don't think she's recovered from it all and, to be honest, I don't think I have either.

We walk into a club called Eleven and music literally vibrates through my body, a thumping beat mixed with various moments from Ke$ha songs. DJs seem to have one mission in life: to give you a headache and to look like douchebags while they do it. The place is packed—a little too packed for a Wednesday at 6 p.m., if you ask me. How does everyone in Los Angeles have so much money and yet so much time on their hands? A very gorgeous Spanish-looking man who is covered in tattoos is dancing in his underwear on the bar. He's wearing a pair of football pads, a black sailor's hat and, believe it or not, he actually pulls it off. I look around the bar at all the beautiful men, men who are far less complicated than Taylor Grayson will ever be, and I try to motivate myself to think of them instead of the man I've been obsessing over all day. It's actually a nice break to be obsessing over Taylor here, instead of what I normally obsess over in bars, which is essentially just an inferiority complex around shirtless abs and pecs. Few things make me as nervous as people with perfect bodies—that's why I don't go to the gym ... also because I'm too lazy to go to the gym.

Josh orders me a drink. I tell him to just get me whatever he's getting himself. I never know what to order in bars. If I order for myself I'll end up being the only guy in the bar who's drinking Pinot Grigio, and I just can't be that guy tonight, not after the past twenty-four hours. Matty arrives looking like he's stepped out of an ad for some sort of gay movie musical, the most over-the-top touch being his *Chorus Line* tank top and green fedora.

'What are you wearing?'

'Do you like it?' Matty says, spinning around to model the rest of the outfit. I don't, but I can't say that to Matty. No one can. Matty is sensitive about these kinds of things, so it's best to always just play along or else you'll spend the better half of the night talking him off the hypothetical ledge. Matty might act like the most confident person in the room, but inside I suspect he's just as fucked up as I am. Maybe even more.

'You look AMAZING!' I shout over the loud crowd and Robyn remix. Josh walks over with our drinks.

'Here you go. I got vodka sodas.' He catches sight of Matty in his ridiculous outfit from the corner of his eye. 'Oh hey, Matty. I'm going to run to the restroom.'

Matty watches Josh walk away, then turns his head to me and whispers, 'He wants you.' I'm just relieved Matty isn't going to complain that Josh didn't compliment his outfit.

'You don't know that,' I tell him, taking a sip from the extremely strong drink. I am right, he doesn't know that, but that doesn't stop the fact that he's probably right.

'Please. He's always staring at you like a sad puppy. Or worse—like a single thirty-five-year-old woman. And how many times has he invited you to dinner?'

Matty's on to something. Josh has been trying to get me to go out with him for months, but I've always had a good excuse. Sick, working, friend in town, Gina Gershon on *Watch What Happens Live*. Somehow though, I've ended up out with him and I wonder for a second if this is all a big plan to get me drunk and take me home with him. Just then, Josh returns and, not helping to disprove my suspicions, he's carrying three tequila shots.

'Shots!' he shouts. Matty cheers.

'I can't do shots. They're too much for me,' I say Matty knows this. They both do. They've seen me drink shots and it does *not* go well. Like, wake up the next morning in someone's car in Sherman Oaks and then vomit for three days while watching a *Long Island Medium* marathon on TLC kind of not well. Before I can protest any further though, Matty has poured the shot down my throat. Admittedly, I don't put up much of a fight. I gag from the taste and it doesn't take long before I'm drunk.

I've definitely loosened up, but I'm still completely uncomfortable and getting a little dizzy. I had been doing a really good job of keeping track of what I was drinking, but now, an hour into our evening I can barely even remember getting here. I've had what? Two vodka sodas and a shot? Or was it three?

Time passes in gay bars in the strangest ways. It's like Alice's Wonderland except with more than one queen. Josh asks me to dance and, without giving me much of a choice, pulls me on to the dance floor. I hate dancing in public, there's really no way not to look ridiculous. Especially for me, I'm over six feet, so when I dance I feel like that octopus sea monster attacking Shelley Duvall in the *Popeye* movie.

'If I'm going to keep dancing,' I slur, 'I'm going to need another drink.'

If there was any question before, there certainly isn't any now ... I'm a hundred per cent, without a doubt, drunk. Even drunk enough to dance all by myself while I wait for Josh. I am having my own personal kiki when I look across the bar and see that he's waiting in line. When he looks at me, he waves and smiles. I could get into Josh, I guess. I imagine him without a shirt and it's not a bad image. He's tall and has a nicely toned body. His long blond hair also makes him look like a sexy Malibu surfer. To most people Josh would be hot, but for me it's just too familiar. I don't see him in that light, I guess, but ... could I?

I finish my vodka soda in one long swig but no matter how drunk I get myself I still can't seem to stop thinking about Taylor. That's when I remember, I've got Taylor's number written on that note in my pocket.

I will admit to not making the best decisions when I'm drunk, but who does? I bought a very expensive original *Oprah Winfrey Show* sweatshirt on eBay the last time I had even one margarita. I should be kept far, far away from any sort of decision right now—big or small.

However, what happens next is undoubtedly a very bad decision. I inch my way through the crowd and get outside. I pull out the note and read it again, for the nine-hundredth time since this morning, and then I pull out my phone and dial the number. It rings, which for some reason surprises me. I don't know what I had expected it to do, but I guess I had assumed that famous people's phones work differently from the phones of us civilians. After two rings, he picks up.

'Hello?' It's him. His voice has a sexy deepness and a very subtle gravelly sound to it. I try to speak but can't.

'Hello?' he says again, sounding a little annoyed and likely assuming I'm a telemarketer or prank caller. I am breathing heavily and I know he can hear me. What's more, I want to speak, but I'm literally vocally paralyzed by the sound of his voice. Finally, after what feels like hours, but has probably only been ten seconds, I reply, 'Hi, it's me. It's ... Alex Kirby. We met at—'

He cuts me off. 'Alex! You called. I'm really glad.'

Glad? He's glad I called. I can't begin to describe the places my mind is going. I'm starting to get hard just—

'Where are you? It's very loud,' he says, sounding concerned.

'I'm in WeHo, West Hollywood. Some friends from work and I went out. God, what time is it?'

'Alex, are you drunk?' Now he sounds even more serious than usual, angry almost. I start to get nervous. Did I say the wrong thing again?

'Yeah, a little. Okay. A lot,' I say, holding myself up against a wall, which begins to spin before my eyes.

'I'm coming to get you. Tell me where you are.'

I can't tell if he's joking. Is he literally coming to West Hollywood to pick my drunk ass up? And more importantly, am I simply hallucinating?

'Tell me where you are, Alex, or I'll come find you myself.' Now there is no question about it, he's angry. But why?

'I'm at Eleven. It's on—'

He hangs up just as Josh comes out of the bar, looking for me.

'There you are.' He's also very drunk. 'I was getting a little worried.'

He comes over to me and wraps his arms around my waist. His breath smells like a combination of liquor, cigarettes and spearmint gum. A weird combination that does not, in any situation, prove to be appealing.

'Come back inside so we can keep dancing,' he says, pulling me toward him. I try to push him away without actually having to push, but he pulls me back close again. He's not being too forward, he's just being drunk. Josh is a sweetheart and doesn't mean any harm, but he's getting a little too aggressive and I'm starting to wish I could just be back at home, watching whatever is taped on my DVR. Which I'm hoping is a new episode of *Nashville*.

'I'm really happy you came out tonight, Alex. I really like you.' He takes my hand. 'I really, really like you.' He looks deep into my eyes and I pull away.

'I actually need to get going.' I have no idea how I'll get home, unless Taylor Grayson is legitimately coming to pick me up which ... why the hell would he do that?

'No. You can't leave yet. You can come home with me. I live right around the corner.'

He's got a big smile on his face and I can tell he's not listening to a word I say. I can also tell he's doing to me what I had just done to him; imagining what I'd look like without my shirt on. He pulls me toward him again and this time I have to push him away, physically, and tell him, 'No!'

He's beginning to protest when a big black SUV pulls up next to us. The windows are tinted in that way that tells you there's a famous person inside. The horn honks and I look over.

'Oh my god! Do you think that's Obama?' Josh says squinting, trying to see through the front windshield.

The window cracks just slightly, enough that you can hear the passenger in the back, but not so far that you can see him. 'Hey, Alex. It's me. Come on!' I can tell who it is, and I cannot believe he really came. Without even a second thought, I run over to the car and get in. Josh watches me go, confused but too drunk to do anything about it.

Once inside, I'm suddenly sitting in the backseat with Taylor, who gives me a bottle of water, two aspirin and an extremely disappointed look. He looks me up and down. I'm sweaty, my hair looks like a rat's nest, and I absolutely reek of alcohol. The seats are very comfortable, so comfortable in fact that the last thing I can remember is Taylor looking up at the driver and calling out, 'Drive.' And then everything fades to black.

CHAPTER 11

WHEN I WAKE UP the next morning, I'm more than a little groggy. Groggy doesn't even begin to cover it. I'm smacked against the wall, room spinning, head throbbing hung over. I also have absolutely no idea where I am. The bed is extremely comfortable, so I know I'm not on my futon at home. There's also the smell of bacon and for a split second I worry that I passed out at the IHOP up the street from the Beverly Center. Again.

As I open my eyes, the sun is aggressively bright, and it takes a moment for my vision to come back, but once it does I see an enormous picture window looking out over Hollywood. It's one of the most cinematic views I've ever seen of Los Angeles, and if it weren't so smoggy you could probably even see the ocean.

I'm just about on the verge of asking out loud, 'Where am I?' when Taylor walks in, sweaty from a workout. He's wearing a pair of green gym shorts that cling to his butt and crotch, both damp with sweat. They hang just a little too low, revealing the top part of a white jockstrap underneath, and he's wearing a grey tank top that clings to his sweaty chest. A green bandana ties his hair back. He looks perfect.

'Good morning,' I manage to get out.

'More like afternoon,' he says pointing to the clock on the wall. Is it actually 1 p.m.? How long have I been sleeping?

'I'm so sorry you had to see me like that last night, Taylor ... I'm normally not—'

He cuts me off before I can finish.

'You were in rare form. Seriously, Alex. I was worried. What did you drink?'

I rub the temples of my forehead. 'All of it.'

Taylor grabs a towel and wipes the sweat off his forehead and tosses the towel into a hamper.

'Well. You've got to be more careful. You could have really hurt yourself.' He begins to stretch his forearms over his head, which are looking especially ripped from the gym. 'And who was that guy outside? The one that was trying to kiss you. Did you even know him?'

My memory is hazy, but then I remember—Josh! I forgot about Josh.

'That was Josh. He's ... a friend ... and a co-worker of mine. He was really drunk too,' I tell him.

He gives me a look as if it to say, 'Ya think?'

'Is this your apartment?' I ask, looking around the immaculate room. It's not just the enormous king sized bed—there's a beautiful red sofa and an oak coffee table. High ceilings with glass light fixtures the shape of diamonds hanging overhead. The place could be the set of a 1940s romantic comedy.

'No, this is a hotel I stay at when I'm in Hollywood. I

have a house out in the Santa Monica mountains but it's a bitch to get to, so if I have to be in Hollywood I stay here. At the Roosevelt.'

'We're at the Roosevelt?!' I ask in shock. A deep panic sets in: did I really go through the Roosevelt Hotel lobby passed out drunk last night? Who am I? Marilyn Monroe?

He laughs. 'Yes. I suppose you don't remember trying to order a nightcap in the bar downstairs.'

I am humiliated. I call Taylor Grayson, and this is how I act? A drunken idiot making an ass of himself in the lobby of the Hollywood Roosevelt Hotel?

'I suppose you also don't remember making out with my publicist, Belinda?'

Belinda? The woman with the *Nightmare Before Christmas* face? Surely, God have mercy, I didn't—

'I'm kidding,' he says with a grin.

I stand up and get immediately dizzy. 'I've got to get going. Matty and Josh are probably freaking out.' I look down at my underwear. 'Where are my pants?'

'They're in the foyer. I had them sent out and laundered this morning. Your shirt however was ... well, it needed to be thrown out.'

Visions of projectile vomiting circle in my head. 'Oh god! Did I throw up on it?' I ask, not really wanting to know.

'No. It was just an ugly shirt.' He winks and takes a swig of his protein shake. 'My driver will take you home whenever you're ready.'

What if I'm not ready? What if I never want to leave again?

'I can't let him do that. I'll just get a cab. You've done enough. Really, I'm very sorry.'

'Absolutely not,' he insists. 'Now get dressed and get going. I've got to get to a meeting. And housekeeping is being impatient about cleaning up the room.'

He slips into the bathroom and shuts the door, I hear the shower turn on. I stand there, imagining his naked body, sweaty from his workout. I imagine him peeling off the grey tank top that's basically glued to his body with sweat, and then the shorts, standing there in just his white jock strap. His perfect ass, his humongous thighs, his broad shoulders—*put on your pants, Alex.*

My pants are folded up neatly on a chair in the foyer sitting next to a large bag from Bloomingdale's. Inside are three different shirts: a T-shirt, a tank top, and a button-up. All for me. I go for the T-shirt. Next I put on my shoes and as I'm tying them, Taylor returns. He is still glistening wet from the quick shower, but in a fresh pair of shorts with no shirt. His chest and stomach literally ripple with muscles. He has a six-pack, yes, but even hotter are his pecs—they're perfect, just the right size and roundness. His chest is hairy but not too much, not too little. His happy trail gets darker and darker the lower it goes, leaving the rest up to the imagination.

'I'd like to see you again,' he tells me, straightforward.

What is this supposed to mean? I have a thousand questions. For one, why does he want to see me? And secondly, will he please just bend me over this chair and fuck me for the next five days?

'But it's complicated,' he adds, 'and I need you to be open to it.'

I'm more confused than ever. So he *is* gay? But closeted? That *is* complicated but it's all beginning to make sense.

'I think I understand.'

'No.' He stares with the usual serious expression. 'I don't think you do. But you will. Very soon.'

At this moment, I'm overcome with an uncharacteristic amount of courage and I ask him, point-blank: 'Are you gay?' His face doesn't shift at all. It's as stone-still as it's been all morning, as it's been since the first moment he ever spoke to me.

'I don't identify as anything. I don't do romance. With men *or* women. So I guess no ... I'm not.' His eyes do not move away from my own. 'I don't do hand holding, movie dates, candlelit dinners, anniversaries, birthdays ...' He's made his point and I'm not sure why he's continuing to outline what he doesn't do. '... but I can't tell you anything else. It will all have to wait.'

Damn. He's all about the build-up with no release. I want to shout 'When?'. I want to grab him and insist he explain everything right this very second, but I manage to keep my cool and simply nod.

'Well, you have my number,' I tell him with a confidence that's as put on as Anne Hathaway's humble facade. He grins, like he grinned at me in the interview, then says 'Oh, fuck it.' The next few moments are hazy as he walks over and grabs my chin. His eyes drill into me as he pulls me toward him and begins to kiss me. His lips are even softer than I imagined, fuck memory foam pillows ... these things are a hundred per cent down. His delicious tongue slips between his lips, then between mine, into my mouth, past my teeth and rests upon my own tongue. Together they taste warm, salty and delicious. We stand in the foyer, kissing, and I want time to stop. I want to be able to step out of my body and look at us standing there, to watch it like I would a scene in one of his movies. This beautiful man holding my face so sweetly and tenderly, kissing me like I've never been kissed before. It's just me and Taylor Grayson. Shirtless. In the Hollywood Roosevelt Hotel. And there's nowhere else in the entire world that I'd rather be.

He pulls away, still grinning. 'Will you have dinner with me tomorrow night?'

I pretend to think about it, like I have to consult a fictional calendar filled with fictional dates and plans. 'Yes. I'd like that.' I take a deep breath. 'I'd like that very much.'

And I would. I really, really would.

CHAPTER 12

THE NEXT TWENTY-FOUR HOURS are ticking by at a snail's pace. I feel like a kid on Christmas Eve, waiting desperately for time to pass so that I can open the presents. That sounds pretty creepy, doesn't it? Besides, this is better than Christmas, this is ... well, it's a non-date with Taylor Grayson, who a mere twelve hours ago stuck his tongue down my throat. So in other words, it's gay Christmas.

However, first I will have to face Matty in my very first walk of shame.

Matty is at home doing what everyone does when they're hung over: he's watching *Here Comes Honey Boo Boo* and eating an omelet. I can hear the TV before I even open the front door. I'm dreading having to face his questioning because I have nothing to tell. Well, I do have *something* to tell but I promised Taylor I wouldn't say anything, and that's a promise I'm going to keep.

'Well, look what Andrew Lloyd Webber's *Cats* dragged in.' Matty pauses the TV. 'I want to know everything. Oh, and by the way, I'm really pissed at you for disappearing like that.'

I explain, or rather lie.

'I was way too drunk. You guys know I can't handle shots and I had to get out of there before I got sick in front of everyone.'

Matty rolls his eyes and hits mute on the remote control. 'Josh has called here like five thousand times.'

Josh. Again, I completely forgot about Josh. Did he see Taylor? Did he say something? Maybe he did, but was so drunk that no one believed him.

'He really wants to apologize for being so aggressive with you,' Matty explains, but I'm not in the headspace to deal with it. I know that Josh was drunk, he's a good guy, he wouldn't do anything to hurt me intentionally. Josh is the type of person who would be devastated at the idea of hurting someone's feelings. But that's not what is important right now. What is important is getting some Advil and then attempting to sleep until it's time to see Taylor again. But before I can get out of the room, Matty tells me he's in love.

'It was like magic. Honestly. His name is Dan and I don't think I've ever felt something this strong before, Alex. It was electric.'

Matty has been in love at least fifty times in the five years we've lived together. With Matty, if love were a pop star, it'd be Celine Dion, in that you think at some point he'll exhaust all the possibilities, but somehow he always manages to keep going. I sometimes wish I could be more like Matty, more capable of falling in love at the drop of a hat.

'And what about you? Did you get ... laid?' Matty might want me to get laid more than I want it, which is really saying something as getting laid has quickly become all I can think about.

'No, Matty. I was a proper lady.'

I walk to my door, and just before I shut it Matty calls back to me: 'Nice new shirt!'

Matty, the Jessica Fletcher of one night stands.

* * *

I'm waiting outside my apartment building for Taylor's car to arrive. Luckily, Matty is out with the aforementioned Dan. Again. They've only known each other for twenty-four hours but in that short time ... they've had sex at least four times (or at least four times that I've heard them), broken up twice, have already said 'I love you' once and have talked about getting a dog but ultimately decided against it.

I'm wearing my cute jeans. I have four pairs of jeans, and none of them are terrible, but these are definitely the cute pair. They're the ones I always wear on job interviews and anywhere I think there might be attractive men. So, because I live in LA, that basically means I wear them every day.

I borrowed a shirt from Matty, who has *much* nicer clothes than I do. I even put a little product in my hair, something I haven't done since maybe ever. My teeth kind of sting from wearing Colgate white strips for more than two hours and I pluck those two brown hairs that show up between my eyebrows on a monthly basis. All in all, I've managed to make myself feel pretty.

With each passing car, my heart skips a beat. A sports car pulls by slowly—it has to be him, I stare into the window and a man my grandfather's age waves at me. I quickly look away and spot the giant black SUV from the night before at the bar. Of course he isn't driving himself, does Taylor Grayson *ever* drive himself? Are famous people even legally allowed to drive in Los Angeles?

The tinted passenger side window rolls down and a driver in a black suit leans over the seat.

'Alex, right?'

I go over to the car, immediately straightening up and walking with the sexiest swagger I can muster.

'Hi, there.' I peek into the backseat, but it's empty. The driver turns his head and waves me inside like he's a secret service agent.

'Hop in. We are heading to Mr Grayson's house.'

I'm confused. I thought Taylor was picking me up, not his driver, but I don't question it. For whatever stupid reason, I've already started to kind of trust Taylor Grayson. So I just get in and off we drive ... to where, I have no idea.

The SUV drives a little outside of Hollywood, past Beverly Hills and on to the freeway. Finally we make our way to the airport—surely, I think to myself, Taylor Grayson doesn't live near the airport. We continue driving down a long road past warehouses, empty fields, an abandoned Office Depot, and finally we reach our destination.

There, in a big open green field, stands Taylor Grayson next to a helicopter. Sitting alone in the back of the car, I say out loud, 'You've got to be kidding me!' Taylor waves as we pull up beside the waiting helicopter. I can't help but think about the scene in *Pretty Woman* where Julia Roberts realizes just how fucking rich Richard Gere is. He opens my car door. Taylor smiles at me.

'Surprise. I live in a helicopter.'

I can tell he's kidding even though he says this with his usual serious straight face. I've never been in a helicopter before, and certainly never met anyone who owns one. He leads me over to the little stairs that lead inside, then takes my hand and helps as I climb in. The inside is much smaller than I had imagined. There are two pilot seats and then another row of seats behind that. However, there's no pilot in sight.

'You sit here. I'll be sitting here.' Taylor says pointing to the pilot's seat.

'You ...' Before I can finish he explains that, yes, he is a licensed helicopter pilot (he even shows me the license to prove it) and that he became one after finding his dream house in the Santa Monica Mountains, which as it turns out, is where we will be having dinner.

'I wanted to live out in the quiet of the wilderness, but it's such a damn hassle to get there in traffic that I decided, why drive when you can fly?'

He's got a point. A ridiculously expensive point.

I climb aboard and buckle in as he turns a key and flips a switch, turning the helicopter on. The SUV is driven away by Taylor's driver, and now we're alone. Just the two of us. He says something, but it's impossible to hear a word he says over the roaring engine. I wonder, for a moment, if he'll kiss me again before we take off. I imagine a sexy romantic kiss before we take off into the air. Something super cinematic and scored by an eighties pop ballad like 'I Think We're

Alone Now'. Suddenly, though, we're airborne, without even the mention of a kiss. We begin to rise into the air and the big green field below gets smaller and smaller. We're off, literally flying across the sky. I can spot a few recognizable buildings below, like a Target ... wait, a Super Target. I get lost in wondering where they've built a Super Target in LA but quickly snap back to reality.

'You okay?' Taylor yells over the engine sounds. I nod. *He* might not think he 'does' romance, but a helicopter ride to a mansion in the mountains is the most romantic thing I've ever experienced in my life—which, admittedly, isn't saying much.

'I love it up here!' he shouts. 'Maybe the most gorgeous view of LA that you can find. If you look way far out your window you'll be able to see Catalina.' I push my face against the glass and he's right, way out in the water sits the tiny island of Catalina, surrounded by the infinite Pacific.

We're flying over the ocean now and I'm doing my best not to think about what would happen if we crashed. If I knew we wouldn't die, I'd be fine with crashing. Just so long as it turned into a *Six Days, Seven Nights* situation, where we're trapped on a deserted island with only our naked bodies to keep each other warm. Not that they were naked in *Six Days, Seven Nights,* but while we're on that topic, why weren't they?

I don't know why I trust this guy so much, so much that I'd let him fly me in a helicopter to some undisclosed location for dinner after meeting him only a week before, but ... I do.

'See that house? Down there?' Taylor points across my

chest out the window, his muscular arm brushing against my stomach as he does it. 'The stone one?' I squint at the dots below, which are beginning to get bigger and bigger as we descend. A moment later I can see it perfectly, but it's not a house. It's not even a mansion. It's an estate.

We arrive on a landing pad, conveniently located in his backyard next to the tennis courts and behind the guest cottage. Somehow, Taylor manages to be as smooth a pilot as he is a flirt, as he opens the hatch and drops the stairs for us to exit the helicopter. He climbs out first and whips his thick dark hair out of his face.

The grounds of the mansion are like nothing I've ever seen. Enormously wide trees fill the yard, which is covered with just about every flower you can imagine. A giant swimming pool with a waterfall spilling into an enormous hot tub stands a few yards to the left; to the right sits the guest cottage that is at least three times the size of my entire apartment building; and directly in front of us towers the house itself. It appears to be at the very least three storeys tall, with all sorts of patios, balconies and windows on every corner. I stand in total and utter awe.

'I hope you're hungry.' Taylor leads us up a path toward the house. 'I'm going to cook for you. Is that alright?'

It occurs to me that I've never had a meal made for me by anyone other than my family, and Matty every once in a while when he buys Hamburger Helper.

We walk into the house, through the kitchen which has most likely at some point served as the cover for *Architectural Digest*. The ceilings are as high as a cathedral, and everything is stained wood and stainless steel. A giant wooden island sits in the middle of the kitchen, stacked with food and cooking supplies.

'I had someone shop for me. Like steak?'

I am barely listening, I'm far more focused on the enormity of the place, and the elegance, and the sexuality. I'm not sure how a house manages to be sexy, but this one does.

'Uh huh,' I reply, without actually knowing what I'm replying to.

'How about you have a seat. I'll get you a glass of wine and we'll catch up while I cook.' Before I can say yes, he pours a glass of Pinot Grigio into a tall wine glass and sits it in front of me. It clinks on the counter top, and the sound echoes throughout the entire room. He turns on some classical music.

'Do you like classical music?' he asks. I can't stand it when people ask me if I like the specific kind of music that is playing underneath the question, because if I say no then I'll look like a jerk. I don't really have an opinion on classical music, other than that it's pretty and I know rich people tend to appreciate it.

'It's pretty,' I answer.

'Strauss,' he throws out, as if I have any idea who that is. I decide to be playful and flirtatious. The way Matty would handle the situation. 'So, tell me, Taylor Grayson, are you like my grandfather or something? Do you *only* listen to old people music?' I smile at him, but he doesn't smile back.

'No. My taste is broad. I like this but I also love pop music and modern stuff. I actually think Ke$ha is interesting. I mean, for someone who mostly sings about getting drunk and making bad choices.'

I quickly tell him the story of going to see her in concert two years ago. We had terrible seats and the woman next to us smelled like canned cat food but it was an amazing night.

'I hear her concerts are great. Never been, but we were on *The Tonight Show* together once.' He chops a giant tomato in half. It's hard to share personal experiences with a celebrity. All I can think about is the kiss and I want to ask him about it, but I'm afraid of coming on too strong. I presume if he wanted, he'd bring it up himself, and since he hasn't, I guess it's safe to assume he's either forgotten about it, wants to forget about it or maybe I just dreamed up the whole thing. But if that's the case, then why am I here?

'I enjoyed our time together yesterday morning.' He doesn't look up but keeps chopping. 'There's something about you, Alex. Something I can't quite put my finger on ... I know I've said this before, but you're really special.' I've now melted, literally melted into a puddle that happens to still look like me sitting in a chair at a kitchen island, but do not be fooled—I am melted!

'After the other day I knew I wanted to spend more serious time with you.'

Serious time? I have no clue what that means, but even if he were to propose marriage to me in this precise moment, I'd probably say yes. And by probably I mean absolutely without a fucking doubt. 'But I'm not sure if you'll be up for it.'

Up for what, I wonder. His fame? I'm fine with fame. In fact, I'm pretty turned on by fame. Sure he's closeted, but that's fine ... so was I for all of highschool and an unfortunate period of 2004.

'I can assure you. I'm very, very up for it,' I say, trying to do my best 'fuck me' smile. Taylor looks up from his chopping and studies my face for a moment.

'Well, let's not get ahead of ourselves.'

He always manages to sound so businesslike, as if we're negotiating a real estate deal or something.

'Tell me about your last relationship,' he says, grinding some pepper into the veggies he's cooking and sipping his wine.

This was the kind of question I was hoping to avoid. Not only have I never had a relationship before, I've never even dated. Not to mention the fact that I'm the only virgin in Los Angeles. I decide to play it cool.

'Tell me about yours first.' I wink at him and he shakes his head no, looking unamused.

'I can't go into any details about my personal life until you sign an NDA. That's a non-disclosure agreement.' He nonchalantly slides a legal document over to me then douses the cooking veggies in olive oil. I look at the important-looking document and it's indeed an NDA. 'I know it sounds odd, but a lot of people would like to screw me over. That comes with the territory of who I am. All my lawyers and publicists are very intense about it. They think I have a lot at stake, so I always have to cover my tracks.'

I've never heard of anyone signing an NDA before, except when Matty auditioned to be on *Big Brother*, but that was different. In this case an NDA, however, doesn't seem too intimidating, especially if it means it will make

Taylor Grayson open up to me—and maybe even let down that serious wall he's got up. I glance over the pages and read a lot of legal words I don't understand.

'Basically it says that you won't tell anyone anything I tell you, and that if you do I can sue you.'

I suppose a responsible person would take this document home and read it over, in depth. Maybe even show it to a lawyer or at the very least someone who went to college. But I'm not responsible and none of my friends went to college. So maybe I'm too eager, maybe I'm desperate for a man to open up to me, maybe I'm already drunk from the glass of Pinot Grigio I just finished, or maybe I just don't care. What's the worst that could happen? I'm sued by Taylor Grayson and he gets, what? *Designing Women* DVD collection? Without giving it another thought, I grab the pen from his hand and sign. He looks up at me.

'Dinner's ready.'

CHAPTER 13

AFTER DINNER, WE MOVE into the living room. There's a fire going in the epic stone fireplace, it's so grand and tall, you could simply walk into it if you were in the mood to set yourself on fire—which I'm not, by the way.

'Well, now that you've signed the agreement we can talk. Openly and honestly.' Taylor leans back in a big leather chair beside the fireplace. *This is it*, I think. *This is the moment where we discuss the kiss*. 'I find you very, very appealing, Alex.' He doesn't look at me, and he doesn't smile.

'I find you very appealing as well.'

He may be the hardest thing I've ever tried to read. And I've even read Suzanne Somers' memoir.

'But I must warn you, before we go any further, that my life is complicated.'

This is like the third time he's said that. What does he mean? Complicated? Are we talking Meryl Streep and Steve Martin in *It's Complicated*? Or are we talking dead bodies in the attic complicated? And more importantly, why are we talking about it? I've signed the agreement, can't he just rip my clothes off now?

'Complicated?' I ask.

'I am very famous.' Taylor says without a trace of ego. 'And my livelihood is tied up in my person. I work for a brand and the brand is Taylor Grayson.'

I can see where this is going. This is where he'll go into his story about being in the closet. A story I don't care to hear—he's closeted, I can't tell anyone we're having sex and seeing each other, fine. I can handle that. Now kiss me.

'I'd like to show you something. Come with me.'

I follow him down a long hallway past photos of him all over the world, a candid shot in someone's backyard with Oprah, a group photo that includes both the President of the United States *and* Tracy Ullman. He has a very weird but cool life.

'What I'm going to show you might surprise you. Which is the main reason I had you sign that NDA. It is vital that what you see stays here. Do you understand?'

'Yes. Tell everyone about what I see,' I joke, but he doesn't laugh. He doesn't even smile.

'This isn't a joke, Alex.'

I blush because his tone sounds like my scolding fifth grade teacher. Instead of attempting to explain my humour and dig myself even further into a hole, I just nod. He opens the door to the room, which is completely dark and walks inside. As he enters, he flips the light switch and a dark, shadowy lamp casts a yellowish light all over the room.

The room is very strange. There is a large four-poster bed with no sheets and with ropes tied to every post. There are rows of other ropes, chains, whips and even riding crops hanging to my left. To my right, there's a swing dangling from a hook on the ceiling. The swing resembles more of a horseback riding saddle, made from black leather with two loops for one's feet. Towering over the bed is a cross configuration. Large enough for a human being. On all four points are straps, seemingly big enough for human hands and feet.

I scan the room, then scan it again, attempting on the second occasion to figure out what the hell all of this means. It looks like a medieval dungeon or just a really crappy furniture store.

'Do you know what this is?' Taylor is watching, waiting for me to speak.

I have absolutely no idea what this is and I'm not even going to pretend to. I shake my head. He smiles and traces his long fingers across the mattress of the bed, then up one of the posts and yanks on the rope. It's tied tight to the bed.

'This is for you, Alex. If you want it.'

I look around the room again. Just *what* is for me? The weird swing? The bed without sheets? The riding crop?

'I'd love to share these things with you. But only if you think it's something you would enjoy as well.'

I nod, still confused out of my mind. 'Do you know what BDSM is?' he asks. I don't. Truth be told, it sounds like a brand of jeans they would sell at H&M.

'Bondage, discipline, sadism, masochism. BDSM.'

I let the words roll around in my mind for a moment and suddenly I understand. He means like S&M sex. Like tie me up, spank me, make me his slave kind of sex. Holy. Shit.

'You're shocked,' he says, not moving his gaze. 'I can tell.'

Well, he's right. Who wouldn't be when the super famous guy they have a crush on tells them they're into the kinkiest of kinky sex?

'If you're scared, if you're uncomfortable, if you are turned off, you can leave this room at any moment. Do you want to go?'

I don't know what to say, and I don't know what I want to do. The voice of responsibility in my head screams: RUN! But I don't listen. Instead, I stay.

'Alright then. Have you ever tried any sort of bondage or S&M before?'

I laugh out loud. I try to keep it in, but I can't. The closest thing to bondage I've ever come is letting a hot guy in Starbucks tie my shoes because I was holding two cups of coffee.

'I'll take that as a no. Well, tell me about your other sexual experiences. I want to get a sense of what you've experienced and what you've liked.' I stare at my feet. Hoping that if I stare down long enough he'll change the subject to something other than my sexual past. Finally, I tell him.

'Well to be honest, I've never ... really had a relationship.'

Taylor nods, seeming to understand completely.

'Okay, but how about people you've fucked? Tell me about them. What did you do?'

He's making this much more difficult than it needs to be, and it's quickly beginning to sound more and more like a job interview.

'Well, that's the thing I've never really ...'

His face scrunches up in a really cute, confused look. I'd find it adorable if I weren't so damn humiliated.

Here comes the conversation I dread anytime it has to be had. No one wants to be anyone's first, they fear it will be too much pressure and they fear that I'll turn into some sort of needy psycho. I've actively avoided this conversation with just about every guy I've ever met, which is why I'm still single and most definitely why I'm still a virgin.

'I'm ... I've never ... you know ... had sex.'

I've come close to having sex, a number of times in fact. I've gone on dates where I could have gone home with the guy. And I've been out where people have propositioned me. One time, this insanely cute guy spent all night complimenting me while I was cater-waitering. He was there as a guest and kept making flirty comments. There was something very sexy about the idea of sneaking off with him during my shift and I even started staking out a location to slip into. He was ready too. He had beautiful olive skin, these hairy toned arms, a skin tight black t-shirt and super dark eyes. He looked sort of like the Greek guy in *The Sisterhood of the Traveling Pants*.

Finally, I found an empty storage closet on the second floor of the party venue and let him know I'd be waiting for him in half an hour. I was prepared to do it when I noticed him with his arm around another very handsome guy. Then I noticed the matching rings on their fingers.

I didn't go up to the second floor to meet him, nor did I tell him I wouldn't be there. Instead, I just left, pitying him, pitying his husband and pitying myself for thinking a connection could be that easy. I'm sure the sex would have been fun, and who knows, maybe they even had an open relationship or something. But I just couldn't let my first time happen so shadily. I guess I've always craved something more like a romantic comedy. Something sweet. Something a bit more Sandra Bullock.

Taylor is looking at me, confused.

'You're a …'

Before he can finish, I nod. I don't want to hear him say the word. It'll be too humiliating. He can't hide the shocked expression on his face as he stares into mine. His expression changes, though, to the look of a wild animal on the verge of attacking. My heart skips a beat as he walks over to me with determination.

'Goddammit! Why didn't you tell me that? I've been standing here, going on and on about all of this and you've never even—' Something shifts in his expression. 'Follow me.'

I follow him as he charges down the hall, up a spiral staircase and into his bedroom. A four-poster bed stands in the middle of his all-white room: white bedding, white dresser, a white desk next to the window with two identical white lamps on either side of the bed. The room is spare and peaceful. Like an Apple store. A giant window looks out over the Pacific Ocean, which bounces little specks of light onto our skin. He turns to me with a quiet casualness.

'We're going to have sex,' he says matter-of-factly.

The waist band to my briefs tightens as my cock automatically stiffens. I start to speak but he puts his hand over my mouth.

'No more talking. Just trust me.'

I don't know why, maybe it's his endless sexual energy or maybe it's the way his strong hands look gripping my waist or maybe it's the fact that he's stupidly famous and that it's true what they say about everyone in Los Angeles being swayed by famous—or let's be honest, it's probably a combination of all the above. Either way, I want to trust him. And, somehow, I do. I don't know why, but I feel like I could trust him with my life.

He pushes me onto the bed. I fall backwards with my eyes fixed on Taylor's face. His hands come to my chest and his long fingers begin to trace my stomach and chest, up and down, up and down. He starts unbuttoning my shirt, starting first with the bottom button, then moving up to the next, then the next. His eyes never shift from mine, he isn't smiling but staring, determined, lost in his own hot sexuality. My shirt is completely unbuttoned and his hands are cold as they move up and down my bare chest. He begins to trace an invisible roadmap with his tongue, starting first at my happy trail and moving up to the middle of my chest, then to my right nipple. He circles it with his tongue, making endless circles of saliva, and then out of nowhere he bites down. I wail in pain and pleasure, it's like nothing I've ever felt before and already I'm eager for him to do it again. His tongue moves to my left nipple, I tense up in excited anticipation. He squeezes my shoulders and whispers: 'Relax.' He then repeats the process on my left nipple, and this time I moan even louder. The pain that shoots through me is an unfamiliar kind of pain, but a pain I could get very used to. He looks up at me, his face a tightened expression of madness, and for the first time all day, he smiles. He leans in and kisses my lips. His tongue slides into my mouth, carefully and calmly, like a hand into a glove. Taylor then grabs the back of my neck and pulls me into him, sliding his tongue deeper and deeper into my mouth, as far as it can possibly go. Without even thinking, I wrap my legs around him and he grabs hold of my butt and cradles me into him.

Finally he pulls away and rips off his own shirt, and I can't help but laugh.

'What is it?' He stares at me, flirtatiously confused.

'I just ... you're so hot it's stupid.'

He grins mysteriously, then backs away for a moment. He removes his big shiny silver watch and places it on a table nearby. He's standing over me, staring down with something sinister in his eyes. I want to grab the back of *his* neck, pull him down to my level again and slide my own tongue into his mouth, but before I can even reach forward he flips me onto my stomach and pins me down with his strong hands.

With one hand he reaches under me and unfastens my jeans. Then using both hands he pulls them off from below. He's masterful at this, pulling off my pants in one fell swoop with no effort on either of our parts. I am now in just my white briefs and socks, laying on my stomach, my eager ass pointing upward. He peels off my socks and begins to massage my toes, hard and unrelenting; even when I cry out in pain, he doesn't stop. In fact, he rubs even harder and deeper. He lowers his mouth onto my toes and begins to suck each of them, one by one.

Taylor's hands move up to my underwear, his fingers tracing the tight stitching of my briefs wrapped around my thighs. He switches from finger to tongue and traces the band that circles my thigh. His tongue almost tickles but

I'm too lost in euphoria to care. He then moves to my other leg. His free hand reaches up to my waistband, slipping into my briefs and around to the front. He grazes my cock lightly with the tips of his fingers and I'm immediately wet with excitement. He leans down and breathes heavily into my ear. His breath is now hot on my neck, and I try to maneuver my mouth to kiss him. Before I can reach him, however, he pulls my underwear down to my ankles, then completely off.

I'm laying completely naked as his tongue makes its way from the bottom of my feet, up my ankles, to the backs of my knees, to my thighs, to the back of my testicles, across my ass crack, all the way up my back and finally to my neck, which he bites so hard I worry he's drawn blood. He flips me around again, at last sliding his mouth onto my cock.

His mouth forms a warm, wet grip around the head of my dick. His lips move down the shaft and back up to the head, teasing the tip with his tongue. Pre-cum begins to bubble from inside me as I try to touch his own briefs, but his hand slaps my arms down and holds them in place. I am lost in the sensation of his mouth on my cock; I cannot believe this is the first time I'm experiencing this. He works my cock up and down and I squirm while he does it. I let out a long moan as he sucks hard and tight, deep-throating the whole thing. My cock is lodged so far down his throat that I can't imagine being able to hold myself back—I feel as though at any second I could climax into his mouth. I want to ask if that's okay, if he'll be upset if I do so, but I can't get the question out. Instead, I continue to cry out and try not come.

He then stands me up and turns me around. He slips his own legs between my thighs and spreads them out, to the point where I'm standing in what looks like that football position where the guy throws the ball to the quarterback. My legs are wide apart and he's holding me close to him, with both his arms wrapped around my chest. I hear the ripping of a foil wrapper and I turn to see him putting on a condom. Then I hear the pop on the lid of a bottle of lube. I try to turn fully, to see his hard cock again but he holds me in place.

Taylor's hands move to my shoulders and his mouth to my right ear. He takes a deep breath and exhales against my neck. 'Ready?' he whispers. I whimper the closest thing to a 'yes' I can muster. He slowly slides a big finger in first and I let out a moan. My ass is as tight as can be and he slides his lubed index finger deeper and deeper into me as I become light-headed with pleasure. The feeling is both excruciating and incredible—as a result my dick gets even harder, something I didn't even know was possible. If one finger hurts this much I can't possibly imagine his entire—wow!—then comes his second finger. With the two fingers now inside of me my ass is ringing in pain and I'm gripping onto the bed, squeezing the sheets between my fingers, holding on for dear life.

I catch a glimpse of Taylor's face. He looks so focused that I can tell that his thoughts are nowhere else in the world except on my asshole.

'If you plan on getting that whole hand in there, I'm going to need at least two Vicodin and some *really* strong pot,' I tell him, but he ignores me. Instead, he slowly slides his fingers out, and my ass quivers as the tips of both his fingers rub against my hole.

I can now feel the head of his cock touching my ass; he rubs the whole thing up and down my ass crack, teasing my hole just slightly. He covers my ass in lube then, taking hold of my shoulders, he slides his cock inside of me. It's slow, first the head, then a bit more, then a bit more, until finally Taylor Grayson's entire cock is filling my asshole.

At first, it is beyond painful. Like, historically bad pain. Like I can understand why some moms resent their kids after childbirth kind of pain. Or why Elton John always seems like he's in a really bad mood kind of pain. Slowly, though, it turns into pleasure. The tension of my asshole begins to loosen, and I start to moan again but moaning doesn't do his enormous cock justice. Instead my moan turns to a yell. I cry out so loudly that I wonder if his neighbours can hear me; then I remember that this he has no neighbours. I cry out again, even louder, the loudest cry of my entire life. I don't care. I don't care who hears me, let the whole world hear me. As Taylor thrusts his cock inside over and over, he reaches around and grabs my cock and begins jerking me off. He continues pumping my ass, and the sharp pain I once felt has turned into complete and utter ecstasy.

Just as I'm beginning to get really comfortable he pulls out and pushes me back onto the bed on my back. We're face to face, his forehead covered in sweat. He spreads my legs wide and enters me again. A similar pain rushes through my ass, then I'm dizzy with pleasure. He thrusts into me and pulls me close at the same time, leaning in to kiss me. My moans are muffled inside of his mouth as our tongues meet and wrap themselves around each other. He rams his cock so far inside of me that all I can do is cry out, my screams vibrating inside of his mouth. His fingers move to my nipples and squeeze them as his one free hand continues to stroke my dick. Forming his fingers into a circle he teases the sensitive tip of my cock, sending me into a pulsating hysteria. I let out another scream, this feels so mind-blowing. Taylor's thrusting turns to jack hammering and he's fucking me so hard the room is spinning. Just then, I feel it, first in my balls, then before I can even say another word cum shoots out of my cock without even being touched. It shoots out large spurts, landing on my stomach, my chest, the bed frame, the sheets, everywhere.

Taylor scoops up my cum with a finger, licking it as he lets out a moan of his own. His already red face turns even redder, and I can feel him orgasm inside me, his cock throbbing, over and over. He seems to come forever.

At last he collapses onto the bed beside me, our bodies soaked in sweat. My head is still spinning and I've almost gone cross-eyed in pleasure. I cannot believe what I've just experienced and I wonder if I'll ever be able to move my body again. And just like that, as Carrie Bradshaw would say, I lost my virginity.

We lie in silence for a while, the only sounds are our heavy breaths. I wipe the sweat from my face and roll over to face him. He looks deeply into my eyes.

'Ever since you walked into that hotel room, I've unable to take you off my mind. You're very special, Alex. Anybody can see it. I'm just lucky I did first.'

The sun has set during our naked wrestling match and

I realize for the first time that the room has become dark. I wonder how late it is, and how long we were making love. Or rather, fucking. We stare up at the ceiling, big white wooden beams crisscross overhead. I drift to sleep, knowing full well that even the best of dream could not compare to what just happened.

CHAPTER 14

WHEN I WAKE UP, the sun is shining behind some thick clouds over the ocean. I look at the clock beside the bed and see it's nine. I wonder for a moment if I've been dreaming, but when I turn and spot Taylor still there beside me, I know that it was far from a dream. After a moment, he opens his eyes.

Taylor smiles. 'Good morning.' He somehow manages to look like a *Men's Vogue* cover model even when just waking up. When he kisses me, I keep my lips closed for fear of my own morning breath. 'Are you hungry?' I'm feeling kind of confident, what with the whole 'I'm not a virgin anymore' thing, so I roll over and grab his shoulder.

'I'm hungry, but not for food.'

He steps out of the bed. 'Nope. That was a one-time thing. You should know that I don't have sex. I fuck. If we did it again right now, it would verge on romantic territory.'

Taylor begins putting on a pair of black briefs that show the outline of his cock.

'Isn't my sleeping over a bit of romantic territory?' I ask him, remembering the heat of his body against me while we slept.

'Another one time thing. Get dressed.'

He tosses me a clean pair of his own underwear and I begin putting them on. I notice that he's watching me.

'May I help you?'

He shakes his head. 'You look very nice in those.'

I look down; I'm wearing a pair of green square cut briefs and he's right, I do look nice.

'You do things to me, Alex.' He walks over to me and gets so close I can feel his breath on my face. Taylor Grayson has no sign of morning breath whatsoever. I'm not surprised. 'You drive me crazy.' I don't tell him that if I've driven *him* crazy then I must be certifiably insane at this point. Instead, I just wink.

He picks me up, literally picks me up, and carries me back over to the bed.

'I thought we were getting food?' I say as I'm being carried across the room in his bulging arms.

'Yes. We were, but that was until I saw you in those briefs.' He drops me down on the bed and walks to his closet.

'What now?'

Silently, he returns from the closet, carrying the same silver necktie he was wearing at his premiere. He grabs my hands and ties them on the bed frame behind my head. I try not to but it's impossible for me to not think of movies like *Saw* and *Hostel*, movies I still regret ever paying twelve dollars to see in the first place. He climbs onto the bed and begins lightly trailing my stomach and chest with his right index finger, and if last night has taught me anything, this is a sign of good things to come. It tickles but it also makes my cock harden.

'How does this feel?'

I try to pull myself out of the tie, but I'm stuck. The knots are as tight as can be.

'A little scary.'

Taylor grins that same grin from last night. 'Scary? Don't you trust me?'

My mind begins to spin—do I trust him? I did last night, enough to let him fuck me into next week.

'Well, let's make you a little more comfortable.'

Taylor pulls down my underwear and slips my erect penis into his mouth. My cock is surrounded by that same warm, wet sensation as before. He begins to suck, moving up and down, taking breaks to lick my balls. His index fingers teases the rim of my sore asshole, it stings from the pain of last night. His cock-sucking gets progressively faster and more intense and just as I'm about to come, he stops and jerks himself off without letting me finish.

'Your orgasm will have to wait. It's time for breakfast.'

I'm literally right on the verge of shooting another enormous load all over myself, and I beg him to let me finish but he simply shakes his head.

'Please! It might fall off it's so hard!' I plead.

'Don't you understand the idea of a dom and sub relationship?'

He asks this with such a matter-of-fact tone that I don't even think to tell him that no, I have absolutely no understanding of this dom and sub relationship. Instead,

I just nod and obey, and I can tell he's pleased because it's the first real smile he's ever shown me. Then we head off to breakfast.

* * *

There's an enormous enclosed patio in his backyard, complete with an outdoor kitchen and even a TV. If I had a TV, a sofa and a refrigerator full of snacks in my backyard, it would be the closest thing to camping I'd probably ever try.

We're both in gym shorts and t-shirts as we make our way down the little stone path leading to his outdoor palace that's almost as big his indoor palace. From anywhere you sit in this patio, you get a bird's eye view of the ocean. The pool is also within view, and it's one of those infinity pools that look like it simply drops off the cliff into the sky.

'We're having eggs,' Taylor says, cracking one open and into a pan he's placed on the stovetop. 'Have a seat. Get comfortable. Would you like some juice?'

'I'd love a coffee,' I tell him, desperately in need of a pick-me-up after the most physically active night of my entire life.

'I don't have coffee. I don't drink it. It's terrible for you. You'll have some juice.'

Before I can even respond, Taylor has poured me a glass of grapefruit juice and placed it in front of me. I consider protesting his stance against coffee but decide it ultimately isn't worth it; if I've learnt one thing about Taylor Grayson, it's that he is very used to getting his way.

'I can be a bit controlling sometimes,' he says.

Something about his off-handedness with the comment really gets to me. How unaware could this guy possibly be? A *bit* controlling? He's already tied me up, come on my chest, refused to let me come in return and then didn't let me drink coffee. I'd say he's a tad beyond 'a bit controlling'.

'Did you enjoy our time together last night?'

'Uh huh,' I say, trying to stifle my annoyance.

'What does "uh huh" mean?' he asks without looking up from the egg whites on the stove.

For a moment, I think I might hate this guy. Sure, he gave me the best night of my life but it's as if no one has ever said no to him before. And what's worse, that's probably the truth.

'I enjoyed it,' he says, locking his gaze into mine. 'I enjoyed it very much.'

My heart rises a little and all traces of annoyance disappear. I'm back to being infatuated with him as I stare into his controlling eyes.

'It means yes, I enjoyed it very much. I'd very much like to do it again.'

I hope I'm not coming across too eager.

'I'd like that too.' He puts the eggs on two plates and brings them over to the table. 'I will be sending over the dom/sub contract later today. I'd love your decision, the sooner the better. I don't know how much longer I can go without fucking you again.'

He can't go more than five minutes without bringing up that damn dom/sub thing. I personally loved the sex we had last night, and there wasn't any contract involved there. Why can't we just do something like that again?

'What is with you and this contract?'

He looks up from his plate, frustrated.

'It's to state in writing that what we do together is mutually agreed upon, so that we both understand that it isn't abuse.'

Abuse? Jesus. This just gets weirder and weirder. I think back to that sex room in his house, the weird poles hanging from the walls, the riding crops, the chains and paddles. This guy means business.

'What got you into this?'

'What? Breakfast?' He doesn't smile, but I can tell he's joking. Why does he have to make this so hard?

'The dom thing.'

He shrugs, as if I've just asked him, 'Why do you drink almond milk?'

'I like it.'

For a guy who makes his living off emoting and talking, he's not always very good at it in real life.

'But, like, how? Why did you get into it?'

He puts down his fork and crosses his hands on the table in front of him, looking up at me.

'I was the sub in a dom/sub relationship when I was twenty.'

I almost spit out my juice. Taylor Grayson? Submissive? The same guy who wouldn't even let me come? I decide to pry a little further.

'It was how I was introduced to sex. So it's what I know, and I know I like it.'

'Who was the ... dom?'

It's hard to say things like dom and sub without making yourself laugh, and if that's not the case then you take life way too seriously.

'My first agent.'

Yikes! Hollywood is just as strange as people say it is.

'It wasn't too weird, though. He wasn't super old or anything. He was really hot and really powerful, and it really turned me on.' He pauses, lost in thought for a moment, reflecting on the past. 'I have him to thank for, well, everything.'

I'm beginning to understand. Taylor Grayson's whole career came about from a dom/sub relationship. One of the biggest Hollywood success stories all leads back to some guy getting whipped while wearing a ball gag? I wonder if Kevin Spacey has the same background.

'Are you still ...'

He looks at me confused.

'Still what? In that relationship? No. Obviously not. I don't have sex with multiple people at once. I'm the only person on earth who still believes in monogamy.'

It's hard to listen to someone who tied me up with a necktie talk about traditional values without rolling my eyes.

'Why are you rolling your eyes?' he asks, looking at my intensely.

'Because ... it's just ... this is isn't something I talk about very much.'

Taylor becomes even more serious than he's been all morning, and that's saying something. 'Well, I'd like us to be able to do that. I really like you, Alex. I really want to pursue this relationship with you, but I can't unless you understand that this is a real thing.'

He's intimidating. One of those people with a quiet intensity that feels like a bomb on the verge of going off. Part of me wonders if this is all an act, yet another quirk in the great scheme of actor quirk, but it can't be. Nobody builds an entire sex room in their house just to be quirky. Not even in Hollywood.

'I hope you'll go home tonight and research all of this further. Get to know the facts and then we can discuss some more. Okay?'

I'm silent. I just nod. Mentally preparing myself for a night of BDSM research.

'Do you think this is something you can give actual serious thought to? Be honest.'

He's staring at me with a cool, calm demeanor but I can tell underneath it he's anxious for an answer. I don't know what to say. Do I actually think I could do this? Do I want to do this? He places his hand on my knee underneath the table. For a moment, it feels like a romantic gesture. Then, it slowly makes its way up to my crotch and then he cups my dick and balls, nixing any trace of romance.

'I so hope you'll strongly consider it.' He removes his hand from my crotch. 'Now eat your eggs.'

I do as I'm told, and within moments see the pleasure it brings to his eyes.

CHAPTER 15

BACK HOME, I'VE got the place to myself. There really is nothing like having the house to yourself when your roommate is essentially Jack from *Will & Grace*, but like ... an even bigger gay stereotype. I love Matty, but as with anyone you consider family, I'd say forty per cent of the time I have to will myself not to murder him.

The apartment is perfectly quiet, perfectly still and perfectly calm. It's one of those gorgeous Los Angeles afternoons where a light chill is blowing in through the window and there's the ongoing whoosh of palm trees swaying in the wind outside.

I spend all day on the couch and even though I hate to admit it, I'm watching Taylor Grayson movies. That said, if anyone asks, I plan on telling them that I went hiking and then had a kale, carrot and beet pressed juice. In each movie, Taylor's face and body seem to get more and more gorgeous. As I lie, beached like a whale on the couch, I can't help but imagine Taylor standing over my tied-up body in the morning. I remember the feeling of his index finger sliding into my ass for the first time, and I slip my hand down my pants as my cock gets hard all over again.

Just then Matty gets home. The credits for Taylor's 2010 romantic comedy *I Like, Like You* are rolling across the screen. The movie is, on the whole, one of his weakest. It's one of those forced romantic comedies that's basically just a rip off *Pretty Woman*, but with a social worker instead of a prostitute and with Kathrine Heigl instead of Julia Roberts.

'I want to know everything.'

Matty doesn't even say hello, but simply plops down on the sofa beside me, throwing his brown leather jacket on the floor next to my feet. 'Is he gay? By all that is holy, please tell me that he is gay!'

I feel myself begin to blush. I'm terrible at keeping secrets.

Matty can almost read my thoughts. 'He is. He's gay. Holy shit, Taylor Grayson is gay.' Matty's voice carries, and we have neighbours. They're Polish Jews who don't speak English or look us directly in the eye, but still, we have neighbours.

'Shhhhhhh!' I wave my hands in front of Matty's mouth, trying to get him to shut up. 'I refuse to tell you anything.'

Matty gets up from the sofa and stomps into the kitchen.

'Fine. Be a dick. See if I care.' He's not gone for more than fifteen seconds when his head pops back in the room. 'Just tell me this. Did you see his dick?'

I make the motion of zipping my mouth, locking it and then throwing away the key.

'I am just going to believe that you two had sex. I can tell something happened because you're smiling more than

I've ever seen you smile since the premiere weekend of *Magic Mike*. When you're ready to talk, you know where to find me.'

Matty sashays out of the room, which is how he always leaves a room by the way; if things had gone a little differently, Matty would be hosting *America's Next Top Model* and Tyra Banks would be just another supermodel with opinions.

I open up my laptop and go to Google. I mentally prepare myself for the research I'm about embark upon. Where do I even begin? Dom/sub? That sounds like a sandwich you'd order at Quizno's. Focus, I tell myself. Though the prospect of Quizno's *does* sound kind of nice.

Just as I begin to type, my phone rings. It's Josh. How the hell do I keep forgetting about Josh? I never returned his six calls after that night at Eleven. 'Hello,' I answer.

'Alex. I'm so glad I reached you. Listen, I'm so sorry about—'

I can't let him humiliate himself with an apology. Josh is far too nice to let him think he hurt someone. He wasn't the jerk, I was. I'm the one who ran off and ditched him because some A-list movie star took me back to his hotel. Arguably, an excuse anyone can understand.

'Josh, it's fine. I get it. We were both really drunk.'

'No,' he protests. 'I really shouldn't have been so bold. I really like you, Alex. I always have.'

I am flattered to hear that someone as nice and cute as Josh likes me, but far too distracted by thoughts of the way Taylor's tongue felt against my asshole to do anything about it.

'I like you too, Josh.'

I know that was probably the wrong thing to say if I'm trying to shut him up, but what other choice did I have? Tell him I don't find him all that sexually compelling, but that he's 'fun'?

'Really?' I can hear the lilt in his voice. It's the same lilt I get anytime Taylor Grayson says my name. 'I'd really like to take you out sometime. To make up for my behaviour the other night. Maybe not drinks ...' He laughs. I join him, because I feel like I'm supposed to and because I have a flashback of stepping on a drag queen's foot as I went out onto the sidewalk at Eleven and she screamed 'Shade!' at me as I walked away.

'Dinner? Tomorrow night?'

I try to come up with an excuse. However, I suck at excuses. I've used the dead grandmother excuse so many times that for it to have been true I ought to have had, like, twenty-eight grandmothers.

'I can't tomorrow. Or this weekend, but maybe sometime next week?' Which everyone knows is code for: no.

'Okay. Sure. Sounds good.' I can hear his tone shift, he sounds disappointed.

'Thanks for answering, Alex. Have a good night.'

He hangs up and for a brief moment I feel guilty for turning him down. Josh has always been nothing but sweet to me. The first time we met while cater-waitering, I dropped a whole tray of empty wine glasses on the floor of the kitchen. I knew I'd get fired, but before I could even say anything, Josh took the blame himself.

My open Google search catches my eye, snapping me out of memory lane. I get back to work.

I start with the most basic question: 'What is BDSM?' A Wikipedia page appears explaining the history of BDSM. I scroll through it, because it's not the history I'm interested in, it's the present. While I scroll I catch words like 'torture', 'pain', 'beating'. I cannot believe what I'm reading, I cannot believe that so many people find this sort of thing fun. More than anything, though, I can't believe just how strongly I'm considering it.

With every new detail, search result, article, piece of information and video I see, I am increasingly shocked. This is some serious stuff. The necktie around my wrists in Taylor's bed was making out under the bleachers after fifth period compared to the stuff I came across. What's more, I recognize many of the tools and devices I'm reading about from Taylor's secret room.

I feel myself becoming overwhelmed already, and as I attempt to re-read an article about caning, I decide that it's best to put the research to rest for the night and go to bed. I'll think about all of this tomorrow, I tell myself. It's a lie, though, because as I drift off to sleep, visions of riding crops and leather paddles, like sugar plums, dance in my head.

CHAPTER 16

THE FIRST THING I see when I wake up is an email on my phone from Dwight Press, the publishing house in New York where I applied for a job as an assistant editor. They work with some of my favourite writers and have published some of my favourite books. I sent them my resumé on a whim a good two months ago, long enough that I'd forgotten about even sending it. The resumé itself didn't have a lot to offer, but I included a few sample articles I'd written for Matty on *The Star Report's* blog and a few of my short stories with absolutely no expectation of ever hearing from them again. Until now.

The email reads:

Dear Alex,

I'm Alicia Potter, a senior editor at Dwight Press. I have recently read your resumé and writing samples. You're a wonderful writer with an extremely distinct voice. I think you might be a great fit for the Dwight Press family.

We've narrowed down our assistant editor search to

two people, and you're at the top of our list. Do you have plans to be in New York anytime soon? If not, would you be available to do an interview via phone?

Looking forward to speaking further.

Very sincerely, Alicia Potter
Senior Editor, Dwight Press

I can barely piece together my thoughts. Dwight Press is my ultimate dreamplace. The kinds of books they publish are the kinds of books I want to write, and the connections I could make there are priceless. I can already picture myself walking to work from the subway, with a Venti coffee in my hand, a leather messenger bag full of manuscripts, and whoops, I spilt a little hot coffee on my hand, but you know what? I don't care. I'm young and I'm in New York! I want to respond with an immediate 'yes, yes, yes!' but I don't. I tell myself to let it simmer in my mind for a bit, think it through and consider the logistics.

One. There is the issue of money—I have none. Moving is expensive and I'm more than a little strapped for cash right now. I'm so strapped for cash I'm not even so sure it's a strap. I'm pretty sure it's more like a brick wall.

Two. There is the fact that I do like Los Angeles. It's a beautiful city and I've created a nice little life for myself here that I genuinely enjoy. Do I really want to trade all that in for the task of starting over from scratch?

Just then my phone lights up. It's a text from Taylor. Three.

His text reads: 'How'd the research go? Drinks tonight to discuss? I'll pick you up at 8. See you then.'

This bugs me. He always does this ... poses something as a question, but then turns around and tells you what to do. It's the same thing his publicist did to me at our interview. Why does he even waste question marks? There are no questions with Taylor. Only commands.

But before even a moment can pass, I've already responded.

'Can't wait.'

* * *

His car arrives at 8 p.m. sharp. One good thing about control freaks is that they're usually on time. I'm wearing the shirt he bought me, not because I think he'll like it but because it's the only thing I have that's clean. He's in the back of the big black SUV again, and as I climb in I hear the pop of a champagne bottle.

'Good evening.' He looks stunning—even more so than usual. He's in a brown fitted suit with slicked back hair and a grey striped shirt.

He hands me a glass of champagne.

'Cheers. To you, Alex.'

We clink glasses and I quickly down my drink before even considering just what I did that was cheers worthy. I'm strangely nervous, as if this were a first date or something. The car begins to move.

'Well, did you do your research?'

'We're just jumping right into this, aren't we?' I say. I'm not surprised. Taylor has the patience of a three-year-old child. It's at once horribly frustrating and adorable.

'I'm a very busy man, Alex. I'm gearing up to start production on my new movie and my life is about to get hectic again. I really like you and I need an answer.'

I hate when he says stuff like, 'I'm a very busy man.' He sounds so pompous and demeaning. However, pompous and demeaning happen to look *really* good on him. This would all be much easier if the question waiting to be answered was whether I'd like to go out with him sometime.

'I did my research, yes.'

He looks at me eagerly. 'And?'

'And ... I'm still not sure. I've had a lot on my mind today.'

He places his hand on my knee and actually looks concerned, though who knows if he's acting, and for a moment I feel the romantic connection I've been so desperately trying to create with him. It somehow feels incredibly comfortable.

'Are you alright?'

'Yes. Yes, I'm totally fine, but I've had a lot to think about. Can I ask you a question?'

'Of course.'

I'm already dreading the question I'm about to ask and even more so the answer, 'How many others have you done this with?'

'This, meaning drink champagne, or this, meaning the dom/sub relationship?' I give him the internationally recognized 'no shit, Sherlock' face.

'Sixteen others.'

I nod, taking in the number. I'm not sure what I expected him to say but sixteen seems high.

'Are you in contact with any of them?'

He shakes his head.

'Why did they all end?'

'Different reasons. Mostly just not a match. Some didn't enjoy the relationships. Others wanted more than I was able to give them.'

This last part strikes me like a punch in the gut. What did these others want that Taylor refused to give? Affection? Kindness? Love? The things I want from him as well? Am I actually capable of a relationship without love? I've never had one *with* love, but I'd like to think that I could.

'I see.'

His stare burns into me. 'You seem disappointed. Why?'

I think about this for a moment—why *am* I disappointed? He's never made me any promises. He's been nothing but brutally honest with me. He's living a lie to the entire world, but at least with me he's comfortable enough to tell the truth. Shouldn't that, in my heart and mind, count for something?

It's not like signing this agreement would cause me any pain or rather any pain I won't enjoy. The sex was mind blowing, and there's something so exciting about being around him. A lot of people would kill to be in my shoes but I'm just not sure the shoes fit.

I think of telling him about the job offer even though I still don't know if I'll take it. A small, spiteful part of me wants to use the offer to my advantage, to negotiate. I want to tell him it's either on my terms or none at all. I want to insist on actual dates, romantic evenings, and breakfasts in bed if I'm going to let him tie me up and slap my ass until it's numb. I want him to open up to me, to be the sweet guy I know that he is underneath all the baggage. His eyes may be brooding and serious, but behind them, I can tell there is an immense softness stronger than any serious facade.

He opens up an alligator skin briefcase, the kind Tom Cruise uses in *The Firm*. It snaps as he opens it. He pulls out a manila envelope.

'Here is the contract. Look it over and make me a list of your hard limits and soft limits, of what you're willing to do or not do. We can discuss any questions you might have tomorrow. Deal?'

Deal? Again with the business terms. It's hard not to feel like a prostitute, or worse, a real estate agent making some sort of important transaction. Why can't he look me in the eye and tell me I'm special again? Then there wouldn't be a question to answer at all.

I nod. 'Deal.'

'Wonderful. Have a nice night, Alex.' He says putting away the briefcase. 'I'm already looking forward to your call.'

The car stops, I look out the window, and we're back in front of my apartment building.

'Did we really just go out to drinks in your car?'

He laughs. 'What can I say? I like being in control of my surroundings.'

I step out of the car, with the contract tucked underneath my arm, and as I shut the door I call back to him.

'No shit.'

CHAPTER 17

MATTY AND I ARE walking back from Commissary, the coffee shop around the corner from us. He's going on and on about the newest guy in his life—this one, he tells me, is the one. The last guy, the one he met at Eleven, has long since disappeared, never to be spoken of again.

'He walks up to me at the gym—and I know what you're thinking, don't meet guys at the gym, but it's different. We didn't even have sex in the sauna,' he says, as if he'd turned down a million dollars or the chance to see Dolly Parton without her wig on. 'But he asked me where the smoothie bar was and I was so entranced by him that I put down my weights and showed him. Then we spent two hours drinking smoothies and talking about how much we both love shabby-chic furniture and the Oregon coastline.'

As a good friend, I do what I'm supposed to do and listen, merely judging him inside my head. Then again, who am I to judge? I have a contract sitting on my dresser that would essentially say it is okay for Taylor Grayson to beat the shit of me three to four times a week, just because I'm desperate to have sex with him.

'What are you doing this afternoon?' I ask, attempting to switch the conversation to something other than Matty's new obsession.

'Mike, the guy from the gym, and I are going on a hike and then I'm helping him pick out a shirt to wear to some work party.' He stops walking and grabs my hand so quickly I almost drop my coffee. 'Honestly. I think I love him.'

I roll my eyes, but then an unsettling thought crosses my mind: would I sound just as ridiculous talking about Taylor?

Back at home, I start to reply to Alicia from Dwight Press, but when I open my computer, the search results for 'BDSM' are still displayed on the screen. Immediately, I start to feel my temples getting hot with the realization that sooner or later I will have to make a decision. That's usually the first sign of one of my freak-outs. It's not as bad as a panic attack, but it's worse than plain old anxiety. The same way *Paranormal Activity 3* wasn't as good as *1* and *2*, but was nowhere near as terrible as *4*. A million of the subconscious voices inside my head shout in unison: Alex Kirby, what the *hell* do you think you're doing?

My subconscious Greek chorus has a point, and a really nice upper vocal register if you ask me. Yes, it isn't every day that a movie star falls for you—but it's also not every day that the movie star is a demented sex weirdo with more issues than Tilda Swinton's kids will someday have! And me, of all people. Me, the twenty-four-year-old virgin. Me, the straight A student with a promising career ahead of him until he moved to Los Angeles and sort of lost track for a few years. Me, the coward—the big, scared coward.

That's the other subconscious voice I'm dealing with,

that devil on my shoulder that's whispering, 'You never do anything exciting, Alex. You're dull with a capital D.' That subconscious voice is my least favourite. It has a really demeaning tone, the way Barbara Walters sounds when she speaks to reality TV show stars.

Maybe it's true. Maybe the whole reason I've been single for so long is that I give off some kind of 'dull' energy. Humans are animals after all. Maybe guys can just smell it on me. The same way you can always tell when someone's been to a Subway because they smell like bio-engineered onions. Maybe the only reason I'm holding back on this whole thing with Taylor is because I *am* a dull coward. Maybe Taylor Grayson is the universe's ultimate gift to me. Freeing me from my shackles of dullness, through ... well, shackling me.

'I don't want to be dull anymore,' I hear myself say out loud, as if I'm in a cheesy tween movie. It feels good so I say it again, this time looking at myself in the mirror to only further the cheese factor. 'I do not want to be dull anymore!'

I stand there looking at myself. Trying to find a sense of confidence and assuredness underneath the layers upon protective layers I've created through the years. I want to step out of my comfort zone, but is this the only way? Can't I just take a salsa dancing class or learn how to speak Chinese? I know, on some level, that yes, I could do any number of those things. Or maybe the simple act of taking the job in New York and moving to a new life in a new city would force me out of my shell.

The only problem now is I can't get Taylor Grayson's face out my mind. Or his chest. Or his arms. Or the way he makes me feel when his hand casually rubs up against me in the car. Or the way it feels when he kisses me, how it feels as if I've stepped into an old romantic movie, that he is mine and I am his. Or the way it feels when my hands are tied behind my head and he's sucking my cock so hard I wonder if it might fall off.

However, he isn't really mine. Not fully. Sure, we'd be monogamous and having great sex. Sure, he's the one who's eager to solidify our relationship. But it's the relationship itself that leaves me feeling empty. He will never be capable of fully being there for me, not in the way I've imagined someone being there. Not in the way I'd like to believe I deserve.

I feel a tear form in my eye just as there's a knock on my door.

'Just a minute.'

I get up and crack the door open. It's Matty. 'Are you okay in there?'

I nod, hoping he'll go away.

'Have you been crying?'

I rub my eyes, trying to make it seem like I'm just tired. 'No, why?'

'Look at your face.'

I turn and see my reflection. My eyes are puffy and there's the distinct redness and dampness of someone who's spent the past fifteen minutes analysing why the man he has fallen for isn't capable of giving him anything more than a very intense sexual relationship.

'I've just been a little overwhelmed all day.'

This is the same line I used on Taylor. Maybe this time, it'll work better.

'With what?'

I then remember the reason it doesn't work: because there's always that follow-up question where I'm forced to try and explain myself. That's when I blurt out, 'I got a job offer. Well, a potential job offer. It's down to me and one other person.'

Matty grabs me and gives me a big, tight hug. It feels good to be held by someone that I know, without a doubt, cares about me.

'Oh my god! You did? Where? When? Doing what?'

Matty somehow manages to have more energy at 10 p.m. than I'm capable of having all day long.

'Dwight Press. The publishing house, there's an assistant editor position—'

'Assistant editor? Oh my god! Alex, this is huge.' He grabs me by the hand and leads me to the sofa in the living room. 'When do you go? God. I'm going to miss you. Tell me everything, and also move to the West Village so you can be like Carrie Bradshaw!'

'I haven't decided if I would even take it yet.' Matty looks at me, his face shifting from excited to confused.

'Well, you're going to take it, right? I mean, assuming you get it?'

I think of Taylor. I see him, with his thick wavy hair blowing past his eyes in the ocean breeze, as we sat in his backyard eating breakfast. I think of his hand on my knee underneath the table. I think of the necktie, tightly binding my hands to the bed frame.

'What's wrong?'

Matty can read me by my face. He's like a gay Dr Phil, but nice and without seventies facial hair.

'Who is he? Is it Josh? Look, Josh is a Libra, and not even a good one.'

I wish it were Josh. If it were Josh, this wouldn't be so hard. If it were Josh, I probably would already have a bag packed and a Metro card by now.

'It's not Josh. Josh is great but he's—'

Matty grabs his heart as if he's gone into cardiac arrest—I would be concerned if this weren't the same way he reacts anytime Ryan Gosling appears on TV. 'Oh my god. I know who it is!' I can tell from his expression that he most likely does, but I still can't let him say it.

'It's—'

'It's nobody. Or I can't tell you who it is because ... well, it's complicated.'

Matty stares at me. I can tell he's shocked and a little jealous. For once, Matty is jealous *of me*. He shakes his head in disbelief. 'Well, whoever it is. Congrats. But you aren't honestly thinking about giving up this opportunity for some guy, are you?'

That's the problem. Taylor isn't just some guy, he's Taylor fucking Grayson! You don't just walk away from that to become an assistant editor. He's got a People's Choice Award for crying out loud!

'I don't know. That's what I'm trying to decide.'

Matty puts his arm around me and looks me in the eye. 'Alex, I know this may be your first real taste of romance—'

Romance? That's the one thing I know I won't be getting.

'—and I know that you're excited about this guy, and if it's who I think it is, I totally understand why. He's insanely hot and I'm sure he's showering you with all sorts of gifts.'

Does light BDSM count as a gift? I guess it depends on the culture and/or holiday.

'But you can't do this. You can't give up what you've been working toward for somebody else. You just can't. You barely even know him and you're too talented to pass this up. What if he's secretly insane or something?'

Matty doesn't get it. Taylor's not secretly insane, I *know* he's insane. He's put all his flaws on the table for me to see. I know he's into some very out there stuff, I know he doesn't like romance; I know that he likes me but has a weird way of showing it, and I know I really, really like him. There aren't any secrets. There can't be because I already know the biggest ones already.

'Matty, I can make up my own mind. I don't need to always be told what to do. Okay?'

It comes out of me before I can even consider how bitchy I sound. I wasn't trying to have an attitude, I was just trying to make my point—but I got caught up in my own mess. I don't think it was Matty I meant to say this to.

Matty doesn't know this though, and I can see the hurt register on his face.

'That came out more aggressively than it was meant to,' I say, but as he crosses his arms I know he's upset.

'I was trying to help,' he says. 'Just because you've spent your twenties being some wannabe writer lying around the apartment, only talking about going on dates but being too scared to ever actually do it, doesn't mean the rest of us have as well. So maybe if you could listen for just a minute, you'd realize I've been there and could help.'

Matty's words sting. I know he's angry but it all feels a little too far. He has always liked to be an authority on sex in our house, because he thinks he knows everything there is to know about it. A wannabe writer, though? Too scared to do anything? I didn't mean to hurt Matty's feelings, but that's exactly what he's trying to do to me.

Before I can say another word, he's left the room. A few minutes ago, I might have run after him to apologize, but now, after that dig, I think I'll stay exactly where I am.

CHAPTER 18

'HEY.' MATTY IS STANDING over my bed. I can tell from the way the sun hits the *First Wives Club* poster on my wall that it's early morning. I have not slept well, and my neck hurts from all the tossing and turning. 'Somebody is here for you.'

I sit up. I can tell from Matty's tone of voice that he's still angry with me.

'Who?'

'Some guy. He's got a delivery for you. He's waiting in the living room. I've got to get to work.'

Matty turns and is about to walk out of the room without waiting for my response.

'Hey, Matty?'

He snaps his head around and gives me a look of death. The intensity catches me off guard because it's a little much.

'Never mind. Nothing.'

Matty rolls his eyes and leaves. Maybe this New York job thing couldn't have come at a better time. Matty and I have been roommates for so long that it's slowly become a bit toxic. There's a reason I only see my sister twice a year, and that's because I like to avoid the kind of sensitive bitchiness that's now developed between Matty and me.

Taylor's driver, Paul, is standing in our living room. His giant, broad shoulders and three-piece suit look so out of place in our cramped, outdated two-bedroom apartment where the TV is playing an old episode of *Veronica's Closet* on the TV Guide Channel.

'What are you doing here?'

He stands up, as if I'm some sort of foreign dignitary or Adele.

'Mr Grayson wanted me to make sure you got these.'

His face never moves, not a smile or a frown. He hands me a set of car keys.

'Are these car keys?'

He nods.

'But to what? Why?'

He shrugs, hands me an envelope, then leaves, almost having to duck his enormous frame through our front door. I close it behind him and immediately tear open the envelope. Inside is a card with Taylor's initials printed in fancy calligraphy. The card reads:

Dear Alex,

You're the first person I've ever met who rides the bus in LA. And I'd prefer you be the last as well. Here's a gift. It's parked right outside. I hope you enjoy.

Sincerely, TG

I drop the card and run out the front door, still barefoot and in pyjama pants that have polar bears printed on them. There, parked right in front of my apartment building, is a bright red brand new Volkswagen Jetta. I click the remote on my new set of keys and the Jetta lights up and honks. Holy shit! He bought me a car.

* * *

There's no way I can keep this. Absolutely no way whatsoever, no question, nope, forget it.

But it *is* a really cute car. Like, *really* cute.

When I was growing up, all the rich kids in my town drove Jettas, while I had to borrow my mom's 1982 Volvo station wagon if I ever wanted to go anywhere. This Jetta, however, isn't just adorable on the outside—it's got everything. I get inside and find a GPS, seat warmers, built-in Sirius radio, an iPod connector. Even a sunroof!

I can already see myself driving down Sunset Boulevard, windows down, hair blowing in the wind, *The Best of Bette* blaring from the speakers like I don't even care. No more buses, no more smelly, loud drunk guys with a billion bags from Target, no more angry old women who scream at you for the size of your backpack, no more arguing over the twenty cents I'm always short for bus fare.

But I can't take it, the car's too much. Way too expensive and way too much pressure. If I take this thing I will be indebted to Taylor forever. What does he do to people who are indebted to him? If the way he wants to treat me now, before I owe him anything, is any indication, then I do *not* want to find out. This is getting too weird and manipulative. He knows I'm still debating this contract and this is his weird, fucked up way of giving me an incentive.

Well, Taylor Grayson, this is *not* one of my soft limits. This is most certainly a very, very hard limit. I have no choice but to return the car to him.

I will drive out to his house in the mountains of Malibu, give him back the keys, say thanks but no thanks and walk away. Literally walk, by the way, as I will no longer have a car, but I'm not going dwell on that right now. For now, I will give this car back to Taylor Grayson.

He calls me on my way over. My phone rings through the speakers of my car, automatically muting the radio. I don't even know how to work this car yet so I slap a bunch of buttons and finally Taylor's voice surrounds me from all the speakers.

'How does she drive?'

I've never understood why people call cars by female pronouns. It makes about as much sense to me as people who find Anne Hathaway endearing.

'Taylor, I'm on my way to your house.'

He pauses. 'With the signed contract?'

'No, with ... well, we can discuss it when I get there.'

I don't want to say too much on the phone. I know how good he is at talking people out of things and I'm a man on a mission.

'I look forward to seeing you.'

He hangs up. My mind analyses the past ten seconds for the rest of the drive there, while the contract continues to burn a hole in my backpack. As for the car, by the way, she drives beautifully.

* * *

Before I'm even out of the car, Taylor comes out to his front porch.

'You made great time.'

He looks wonderful, of course, but I will not be distracted by a perfectly beautiful man in a light blue tank top.

'We need to talk.'

'Come on in,' he says, opening the door and following behind me into the house.

'I can't accept this.' My adrenaline is running high.

'Accept what?'

'This.' I put the keys in his hand. 'It's too much.'

He looks down at the keys and shakes his head disapprovingly.

'Alex, I wanted to do this. I like giving people gifts.'

'No. The answer is no. I can't. I need you to hear me on this.'

It's as if he isn't listening, and I somehow doubt he is.

'You can't take the bus forever.'

He says this as if I like taking the bus, like he's trying to wean me off eating peanut butter out of the jar at 3 a.m. or watching *Vanderpump Rules*.

'Well, first of all, actually, I can.' He rolls his eyes. 'And even so, this is not the way I want to get a car.'

'What? From your friend who cares about you?' He takes me by the shoulders, his hands gripping me tight. 'It isn't safe to ride the bus at night like you do. You have to stop defying me, Alex.' His eyes are widen with intensity. 'It's as if you *want* to upset me.'

'That's not true! I care so much about you. That's why I can't take the car. It's just not fair. Who knows if I'll ever be able to repay you?' I actually have a sense of when I'll be able to repay him, and it's the twelfth of fucking never.

'I don't want you to repay me—'

'Yes, but I do. And I don't know when I can, so I just want you to keep it—'

He takes my hand.

'But I don't need another car.'

I pull away. 'Then you shouldn't have bought it!'

He grabs my hand again, this time tighter and more aggressive. He yanks me over to him and I fall into his chest. He grabs me by the shoulders and pulls my face against him. He speaks, furious and soft, into my hair.

'Listen. You *will* take this car. You *will* love it. You will appreciate it. And you *will* never worry about repaying me. Do you understand?'

I try to pull away. 'No, I won't—'

His grip tightens and he yanks my face up to his. His eyes are crazy, the same way they looked when he tied my hands with that necktie. 'You need a lesson in obeying me, Mr Kirby. You need a lesson as soon as possible.' Again, I try to wiggle myself out of his clutch, but it doesn't work, he's beyond strong. 'I think it's time you're given that lesson.'

I can't move out of his grip. He is too in control. I want to give myself over to him. Let him give me whatever lessons he wants, but I can't ... I *must* resist ...

'Do you want a lesson? A lesson on obeying, Alex?' His eyes never blink. They drill into my own as I shake my head and grunt out, 'No!' He grabs my mouth and squeezes it tight. It hurts and my jaw tightens, and he begins to kiss me. His kisses are hard and fast, and my body weakens in his arms.

'I am going to ask you again. Do you want a lesson in obeying, Alex?'

I am trying my best to show him nothing. To have one of those stoic, cold faces that nobody can read. Like Gwenyth Paltrow. Except less annoying and pretentious. What does Gwenyth Paltrow have to be stoic about anyway?

I am trying to hide the feelings that I'm having inside, but it's impossible. He's completely irresistible and before I know it I'm saying, 'Yes.'

His face changes and beyond his stoicism, I can tell he's excited. He picks me up and carries me in his arms, down the hall, past the kitchen, up the stairs, all the while continuing to kiss me. Any time my mind begins to question what the hell I'm doing here, it's answered by his kisses. He kicks open the door to his secret room. We go in, and he slams the door behind us.

He tosses me onto the bed and I land on my stomach. With one fell swoop he rips my pants down to my ankles then completely off, tossing them into a corner. He then grabs my right leg and fastens it into a black leather loop hanging on the end of the bed. It's tight and there's no way of getting my ankle out of it. As I attempt to wiggle out, Taylor grabs my other leg and fastens them too. My ankles are now stuck.

He licks my right leg, all the way up past my crotch, grazing the side of my dick, up my stomach, to my neck. He bites it, and I yell in pain. I'm lost in the sensation that is at once fear and pleasure. I try to push him away with my free hand, but he's too strong. Before long, both of my hands are bound and my body forms a wide open X on the bed. I feel completely in his control and in that moment, I let go, I surrender to his touch.

He then walks, slowly, across the room to the shelves of whips, canes, poles, chains and an array of other objects I shiver to imagine the uses of. I am surprised to find that I am not scared but excited about the possibilities that await me.

'What do you think, Alex? A whip?' he asks as casually as you'd offer someone Earl Grey tea.

I don't respond, lost in the moment, but he asks again, this time louder and more forceful.

'I said what do you think, Alex? The whip?' He cracks the whip. The snap of the leather makes me jump.

'Now, this might hurt. Do you realize that?'

I nod, unable to speak.

'I need an answer first.'

'Yes.'

'Yes, who?'

'Yes, sir!' I shout. I can tell this pleases him.

'Very well. One, two, three, fo—' before he even finishes four I hear the whoosh of air behind me and then the pulsating SMACK of the riding crop against my bare skin. My ass immediately stings. I feel punished but rewarded. One half of my brain of is dreading the next smack but the other half is begging for it.

'Do you like that, Alex?'

The crop comes down again, this time a harder and I cry out in pain. The sharp stings make my ass tremble with agony and delight.

'Your ass is so red, Alex. Do you need me to make it feel better?'

Without my having to respond, he knows what I need. Taylor leans down and begins to gently massage my very sore ass. He begins to kiss it, moving his lips up and down and landing eventually in my crack. He rims me, his tongue sharp and narrow on my asshole. I moan and any tension disappears as the tip of his tongue circles my eager asshole. Just as my asshole begins to quiver, he smacks me again, this time the hardest of all. I let out a long cry and see the pleasure it brings to his face.

He quickly unties my feet, then my arms. I could get up and run away in this moment. I could run out the door and never look back. Move to New York, forget I ever met Taylor Grayson and go on to be a famous writer who someday will tell his fabulous writer friends about the weirdest movie star in the world. But I don't. I just stay put and tell myself this is just one last time. The final hurrah.

He undoes the restraints, picks me up once more and carries me over to a wall. I feel limp and weightless in his arms. He pushes me down onto my knees in front of him, and taking hold of my hands he forces me to unzip his pants and pull out his penis. Grabbing the back of my head he forces his hard beautiful cock into my mouth. He begins pounding it in and out. I try not to gag, but as I do, I accidentally bite down. Taylor yelps.

'Oh! Playful are we?' he says with a grin, as he continues to pound his penis in and out of my mouth. Turned on, I reach down to take out my own dick but he slaps my hands away. 'Keep your hands to your side or I'll get the handcuffs,' he growls. I obey, my dick rock-hard, beginning to throb.

Taylor thrusts himself into me faster and faster, and I taste his precum in my mouth. His low moans get louder and louder the faster he goes. He begins to gasp for air as he lodges his cock down my throat. Then I feel it, an explosion in my mouth, hot and wet, I swallow it. All of it, I swallow every last drop.

Then I grab my own dick and finish myself off with only two quick tugs. Cum shoots out of my cock in a series of blasts, landing all over Taylor's feet and floor. He stands above watching me the whole time, and I can feel my heart racing faster than it's ever raced before. Once I'm spent, I grab hold of his meaty thighs and grip them with all my might, then collapse into the puddle of my own semen on the floor.

Taylor lays down on the floor beside me, in silence, as we catch our breaths. We're sticky and wet, and the room smells of sex. I want to tell him how great he made me feel, but that I need more than just sex. That if he actually cares about me like he says, he would want more than just sex too.

I place my hand on his knee. He jerks it away then stands up.

'There are towels in the closet. I'm going to shower.' Taylor puts on a white bathrobe over his sweaty body and ties it shut, his still-erect penis poking through.

I feel ... how do I feel? Exhausted for one—that was

more cardio than I've had since the Scissor Sisters played 'Let's Have a Kiki' at their concert last summer.

The euphoric feelings of being with Taylor disappear quickly as I realize that sex really is the most he can offer me. Somewhere deep down, I thought that maybe by seeing me overcome my own fears he might be able to overcome his.

'Why did you move just now?' I ask as he puts away the sex props. Taylor looks at me, confused. I can't stop replaying the moment where I placed my hand on his knee and the moment he pushed it away. 'When I touched your knee. You moved away. Why?' I ask.

'You know why, Alex. You know I don't do romance and—'

I can't let him continue. Nor can I sit here and listen to this again.

'No, I don't know why. I don't know why you would do everything we just did, give me gifts, buy me dinner, buy me a goddamn car, but then when I try to put my hand on your knee, you push me away! You are so fucked up!'

Taylor stares at me blankly for a moment. He doesn't move.

'Do you think I don't know that? I'm fucked up, Alex. Very, very fucked up.'

He says nothing as he leaves the room. As if telling me he doesn't do romance is perfectly normal, as if that answers everything. I sit there alone in the land of misfit sex toys. And for a split second I think I'm going to cry. Instead though, I get up, clean myself off with a towel, then slip on my pants and go downstairs. I spot the car keys, still sitting on a table. I stare at them and contemplate just taking the keys, leaving and never speaking to Taylor ever again.

'Take the car and go if that's what you're thinking.' His voice startles me. I turn around and he's standing on the stairs, his freshly showered hair slicked back and glistening in the light. 'It's yours after all.'

I have the urge to grab him and shout that he can't keep doing this to me. That I can't have sex with someone I like this much—and who likes me this much—but not express feelings. No one can do that. I want to tell him that he can't spend his life getting only what *he* wants. That at some point he'll have to open up, compromise, let someone in—so why not me?

Instead I say simply, 'I'm going home.'

Taylor walks down the stairs me. 'Alright. In your car?'

I want to take the car, out of spite and anger. But that's the worst possible idea. If I take the car, I'm defeating my point entirely.

'No, I'll take the bus.'

Taylor goes to pick up the keys. 'You can't catch a bus out here. That's the whole reason people live here, because it's so fucking hard to get to. Paul will drive you. He's waiting in the SUV.'

Taylor opens the front door for me and stands there, holding it open.

'Okay, fine,' I tell him, and walk out the door without looking at him. This is it. I'm done. The end. I want him to know how upset I am and I worry that if I do look at him, that if I even catch just a glimpse, that I'll never leave.

That I'll turn around and stay forever. I will myself to keep moving.

I walk across the driveway and get into the black SUV.

'Take me home,' I tell Paul, who nods. We drive off, leaving Taylor standing on his front porch watching me go and, for the first time since walking out the door, I turn around. He's still standing there on his front steps, beautiful against the backdrop of his immaculate house. As we drive further down his long driveway, Taylor becomes just a beautiful silhouette, getting smaller and smaller.

On the ride home, Josh calls. Usually I'd let the call go to voicemail. That's basically how I field all calls unless they're from a New York City area code, in which case I answer because I automatically assume it's Broadway. Which, by the way, it's never been. But after all that's gone down with Taylor, I could use a friendly voice.

'Hello?'

'Alex, it's Josh! How's it going?'

His voice is sweet, so easy to talk to, so kind. The type of voice they'd give to the sweet best friend on a children's cartoon show. It's comforting to hear.

'I'm okay, Josh. What's up?'

I hope he can't tell that I'm upset. I am hardly in the mood to talk about my day.

'I have free tickets to see Carole King at the Hollywood Bowl. They're not great seats but the Bowl is always fun.'

Normally I'd tell him no, but again, today is a new day. So why not? I love the Hollywood Bowl. I love Carole King. Plus this could be the perfect, uncomplicated evening I so badly need to get my mind off of everything with Taylor. 'Sure, that sounds great!'

I can hear the shift in Josh's voice. I have just made his day. Maybe his month. 'Awesome! I will come pick you up. Let's say six-thirty. Can't wait!'

CHAPTER 19

THE HOLLYWOOD BOWL IS magical. I don't care who is playing. Juliana Margulies could get up there and recite Shel Silverstein poems for four and a half hours, and it'd still be an amazing night under the stars. In fact, I'd probably pay an obscene amount of money so that I wouldn't have to see that.

Josh and I take our seats in literally the very last row. The place is packed and Josh has brought a picnic basket with a bottle of wine, fancy cheese, crackers, and cookies.

'Are these homemade?' I say, peeking under the foil that's wrapped around the plate of cookies. Josh blushes as he nods. 'Well la de dah, Martha Stewart.'

'Oh, I'm hardly Martha Stewart,' Josh laughs. 'In fact, when I left my apartment, my kitchen looked like the scene of the Manson murders.'

I give him a justifiably weird look.

'But with chocolate instead of blood.' He looks down at the ground, laughing nervously, then back up 'This just got really weird, didn't it?'

I can tell he's all kinds of nervous but his tension releases as I laugh. One of those great big belly laughs that comes from some hidden joyful part of you that you wish you could easily access on the days where you wake up feeling like you don't matter. Josh opens the bottle of wine and pours it into two plastic wine cups.

'Well, cheers, Alex. To ... um ... Carole King!' Josh clinks his cup with mine and a little wine spills. I can see that for Josh this is a date, maybe even a first date. I suddenly feel a lot of pressure to make sure it goes perfectly, to please him by controlling the situation. God, Taylor Grayson is really rubbing off on me.

Just as the sun goes completely down, Carole King takes the stage and performs her greatest hits, some weird new songs I've never heard and a few covers. She sounds wonderful. Josh and I make small talk throughout and I enjoy the long pauses of silence when we run out of things to say and simply listen to the music.

Some people you just click with and some people you don't. It's the great order of things or the stars or something like that. I suppose falling in love is finding that one person who can appreciate and understand why you want the things you want and do the things you do. I'm trying to understand Taylor. He just isn't trying to understand me.

I don't click with Josh, not romantically at least. I don't know why. On the surface, I should. I find him very cute, funny, sweet, but there's just no excitement. There's none of that rush I get from seeing Taylor's face or smelling the way he smells after a shower. With each passing minute my night goes from the uncomplicated evening I was hoping for to sitting there and wishing I were with Taylor.

After the concert, Josh drives me home. We both sing along to the Carole King album he's got on his iPod and I am so off-key that Josh asks me to stop.

'Wow, you're not much of a singer, are you?' he asks jokingly. He's right, though, I am a *terrible* singer. There's a karaoke bar in Koreatown that won't even let me in the door after what I did to *Call Me Maybe*.

'Bitch!' I pretend to punch him in the arm and he laughs.

'I had a lot of fun tonight.' He's got that tentative tone of a sixteen-year-old boy asking a girl to prom.

I feel the pressure to agree, so I tell him, 'Me too.' The album has ended and he is awkwardly drumming on the steering wheel to music that isn't playing.

'Sorry if I was awkward or anything tonight. I just really like you, Alex, and I guess I was trying really hard to make everything perfect.' I can't let him continue, his sweetness could give me a diabetic seizure worse than Shelby's in *Steel Magnolias*.

'Can I admit something?' he says, fidgeting with the drawstring on his hoodie as he drives. 'I bought the tickets. I saw on your Facebook that you like Carole King. She's under your favorite music, and when I saw she was coming to the Bowl, I bought tickets. Like, two months ago. I'm sorry, I know it's lame that I didn't tell you. I just didn't want you to think that I was a stalker or something.'

Suddenly I feel terrible, absolutely terrible. He bought the tickets, for *me*?

'Oh my god! Let me pay you for mine. How much was it?'

'No,' he says shaking his head, 'absolutely not. It's my treat. I wanted to do it.'

I look at Josh with admiration. I wish I could like him the way he likes me—this would be so much easier. Taylor buys me a car and he can't let me put my hand on his knee after we have sex. Josh buys me concert tickets and would let me put my hand anywhere I like. Yet I know you can't control your heart, or your brain for that matter. You can't control anything. I just wish somebody could explain that to Taylor Grayson.

'That's very sweet, Josh. And I really appreciate it. I'm treating you to dinner next time we hang out. As a thank you.' Josh lights up. I can tell he heard that as 'second date'. I continue quickly, 'But I'm not really looking to date right now. You're awesome, but if it's okay I'd prefer we just be friends.'

Josh's lit up expression fades. I recognize the look because it's the same expression I had when Taylor pushed my hand away.

'Okay. I get it,' he says, nodding.

'Are you sure?'

'Yeah,' He stares out the driver's window as we stop at a red light and doesn't speak for the rest of the drive home.

When we pull up to my apartment building, we continue to sit in awkward silence. A woman walks by with a small grey dog on a leash. She stops right in front of our now-parked car, and we both pretend to be interested in the dog as it pees on a tree. Then they keep walking.

'You're a great guy, Josh. And someone is going to be very lucky to fall in love with you someday.'

He smiles. 'Thanks.' I can still see the disappointment behind it though.

I unbuckle my seatbelt and open the car door. 'Thanks again for the great night.'

'You too.' He looks at me briefly, but doesn't make direct eye contact. I step out of the car and shut the door. As I walk up the sidewalk, I turn to wave goodbye as he pulls away. He waves but it's a sad little wave as he leaves.

I walk inside, wondering if Taylor Grayson spent his evening thinking about me even half as much as I've thought about him.

When I crawl into bed, all I can think about is how sweet and simple Josh is. How uncomplicated the night had been, despite our weird goodbye. Concert, fun, home. That's a date. Not receive a car, get tied up, have hardcore kinky sex. Life, as Josh just showed me, doesn't have to be so complicated. For all the Taylor Graysons in the world there are dozens of Joshes—but that's the thing. There are lots of Joshes but only one Taylor Grayson. He, no matter how he treats me, is one of a kind.

CHAPTER 20

THAT NIGHT, I HAVE another dream about Taylor. This one, though, isn't sexual. We're at my apartment, not his mansion. We're sitting in the living room and I've ordered Thai food. Red curry with chicken and brown rice with some spring rolls. We're going through the DVR, deleting things we've already watched.

'Is this one yours?' I ask.

'Yeah, but go ahead and delete it,' he tells me, and we repeat this process over and over. We're sitting really close, with my legs draped over his lap. He has his arm around my shoulders and every so often he rubs them, soft and sweet.

He gets up and comes back from the freezer with two pints of Ben and Jerry's. One is New York Super Fudge Chunk, the other is Peanut Butter and Banana Greek Yogurt. We share them, with two spoons, passing the ice cream back and forth. Then lying there in the glow of some show we aren't even paying attention to, we fall asleep.

Just before we doze off and just before the dream ends, Taylor looks up at me and says, 'I'm ready to do this. For real.'

That's when I wake up. I'm not sure what he meant. Do what? Maybe it meant, in the world of the dream at least, that he was ready to open up to me. Or maybe if I hadn't woken up I would have discovered that what he was ready to do was tie me up and stick his dick in my mouth all over again. But something in my gut tells me this isn't the case. It tells me not to give up, because there is something more.

I lie in bed, thinking about how I need to email Alicia at Dwight Press. It's been two days and I think I've made my decision. All signs from the universe are pointing to 'yes', so why not follow? There's nothing keeping me here. Not anymore. Matty and I are barely speaking, I've ruined my friendship with Josh, and Taylor is ... well, Taylor. I'm ready to do it—I'm ready to move to New York.

I roll over in bed and grab my computer. I open up my email to write Alicia but suddenly freeze. There on the screen is a message from Taylor:

'Pick you up at 8? Will explain in the car.'

I stare at the message for a while. My subconscious, the responsible voice that sounds a bit like Miss Honey from *Matilda*, tells me to delete the email. Write Alicia. Then get my ass to New York as fast as I possibly can. But the other voice, the devil on my shoulder voice—the one that sounds like Eartha Kitt but less spooky—whispers: 'Go for it.'

And I obey, because really, who are you going to listen to: Miss Honey or Eartha fucking Kitt?

At eight, Taylor is waiting for me in the car outside the apartment. He's driven the brand new Jetta and as I walk toward the car, he rolls down the window and shouts, 'Great car, huh? Too bad nobody wants it.'

I roll my eyes and get in.

The car smells like his cologne. I don't know what the brand is; maybe it's his own special creation, but whatever it is, it smells like pure unadulterated hotness. I wonder if we'll even discuss the fact that our last time around each other ended in my shouting at him and driving away with tears in my eyes.

'Good evening, Mr Kirby,' he says as I climb in. 'How are you this evening?'

Apparently we will *not* be discussing our last fight. Taylor is being far too smooth and flirtatious for that. I can already tell he's going to pretend like our disagreement never happened. He's going to barrel through in an attempt to get whatever it is he wants. A large part of me wants to force him to talk it through, to demand he apologize and explain his fucked-up mind to me before we go anywhere.

'I'm fine,' I say, friendly but guarded. I'm torn between wanting to display my excitement about seeing him again and wanting to guard my heart so he can't continue to break it. Also, I'd like to punch him in the face. Then kiss it.

'You look nice,' he says, flashing his sparkly eyes over to me. It's hard to stay mad at him with eyes like that. And it's hard to stay guarded around someone so damn charming.

As we pull onto Sunset Boulevard I ask him, 'Where are we going?'

'Dinner,' he says simply as he stares straight ahead.

Dinner with Taylor Grayson could mean anything. It could mean a five-star restaurant in Beverly Hills, it could mean a catered beachside picnic in Malibu, it could mean a helicopter trip upstate to the wine country. It could literally mean anything at all.

'That's vague.'

He glances over at me then back at the road.

'You're going to meet my family.' He makes a left turn onto a residential street in Beverly Hills. The kind of street that only rich people and the folks who clean their houses ever go down.

His family? Is he kidding me? First of all, I've never even imagined Taylor having a family. I just pictured him being created in some sort of movie star-making test tube on the Paramount lot. Beyond that, however, is the fact that I cannot believe Taylor would actually open up so fully as to introduce me to his mom and dad. This seems like a completely uncharacteristic move on the man of mystery's part.

'You're introducing me to your parents?' I say, attempting to mask my shock. While I certainly have my walls up tonight, I can't help but feel a little excited that Taylor is taking this next step. Could this be a good sign? Sure, he can't show me affection, except during our progressively athletic sex, but he's taking a big step, he's opening up in his own weird way. Suddenly I'm feeling that glimmer of hope again.

He laughs and shakes his head. 'No, it's a *much* bigger deal than my parents. I'm introducing you to my agents.'

I roll my eyes, but behind them I realize that this *is* a bigger deal by Hollywood standards. Your agents, especially at Taylor's level, are a part of your every move. Mainly because you're a part of their every dollar.

There are a number of questions I need answered before I can be comfortable meeting these people. For one, how much do they know about Taylor's personal life? How much do they know about me, if anything? And how many of the sixteen others have they met before? Before I can ask any of these questions though, Taylor pulls up a long winding driveway.

I can see the house sitting behind the sprawling lawn ahead. It's one of those tacky castle-looking mansions in Beverly Hills. The kind with giant Greek statues outside. The kind you drive by, peering through the gate, wondering who has the egotistical audacity and money to live in such an over-the-top place. As it turns out, apparently, agents.

'Is there anything I should know?' I ask Taylor, referring mainly to the secret room of pain and the whole 'you're a closeted movie star with a bondage fetish' thing, but without actually having to say that.

He shrugs. 'Just remember, it's LA, so if someone makes you feel fat, it's probably their way of saying that you look better than them.'

As we walk to the front door, I wonder if maybe this whole 'secret room of pain' thing is something everyone in Hollywood has. Maybe everybody who's anybody has a sex dungeon hidden behind the walls of their mansion and shelves of award statuettes—maybe Susan Sarandon is whipping somebody into submission at this very moment. In fact, I don't think anyone would be all that surprised to find that out about Susan Sarandon. I certainly wouldn't.

My nerves are running high, so I'm not thinking straight and as we stand there in silence. I just come out with the question that's been burning on my mind since the first moment we spoke.

'Why me, Taylor?'

He looks over, studying my face for a moment, then rings the doorbell. An obnoxiously loud chime echoes from the inside of the house. You can literally smell money. He turns to face me again.

'Because you're special. That's why.'

An old man with bleached blond hair comes to the door. He's dressed in bright, youthful clothing, as if to distract everyone from the fact that he's seventy-five at the very least.

'Taylor!'

He pulls Taylor into his striped Ralph Lauren Lacrosse-style jersey that would look too youthful on a man even three decades younger than him.

'Come in! Come in! And you must be Alex. I'm Richard Knight.' he says, giving me a friendly knowing smile and shaking my hand with the limpness of a wet noodle or my penis around a naked woman.

I'm pretty shocked that he knows my name, but I try not to show it. Does this mean that Taylor has told him about me? Or is this guy just another professional schmoozer? The Hollywood type who's never sure if you're somebody so he treats you like you are just in case. He ushers us through a nauseatingly grand foyer. Out of the corner of my eye, I notice an oil portrait of Jackie O, clearing up any suspicions that Richard might or might not be a homosexual. The place is done in lots of gold trim and marble. It's the kind of house rich people who think Las Vegas hotel lobbies are the epitome of glamour would build.

'Let's get you two started with cocktails. What can I get you?'

Before I can even speak, Taylor has ordered us two glasses of white wine and we're being ushered into the living room where a handful of people are already situated. I scan the room, each face familiar, gorgeous, and staring at me. The first person I recognize is Belinda, Taylor's publicist. She's giving me a less than friendly glare, but I smile and wave in her direction. Seated on the sofa is a beautiful young blond woman I recognize but can't quite name. It isn't until she stands up and is walking over to me that I realize it's Natalie Nuhause, a Victoria's Secret model turned A-List actress whose movies are consistently both terrible and box office mega-hits. She's even more gorgeous in person, and I'm processing her beauty as she walks over and kisses Taylor on the lips.

'Darling,' she says in one of those pseudo-British accents Americans have after spending three weeks in Europe. 'It's about time you arrived. I've been making small talk with Belinda's husband for the past half an hour and he's yet to look in any direction but my chest.' She waves at Belinda's scrawny, weasel-like husband across the room; he's sitting on the couch in an offensively bright green cardigan and he winks at her. 'Fucking kill me,' I can hear her whisper under her breath.

Taylor laughs and she places her hand on his lower back. He doesn't move away, instead he moves his own hand to her lower back as well and turns to me.

'This is Alex. Alex, this is Natalie.'

She turns to me and smiles so knowingly that I wonder

just what she knows. I'm distracted by the fact that Taylor not only lets Natalie touch him with affection but that he touches her right back.

'Such a pleasure. I've heard a lot about you.' She smiles one of the most fake Hollywood smiles I've ever seen. Okay, so she *clearly* knows I've been spanked. Belinda makes her way over to the three of us and puts her arms around Natalie and Taylor.

'How are my two love birds tonight?'

Taylor's face goes white. I can tell through Belinda's smile that she's enjoying what drama she's just begun to cause.

'Did Taylor tell you? He and Natalie are getting married!'

All of sudden, I'm feeling nauseous. Is this why he brought me here? To humiliate me in front of his friends with the fact that he's getting married? To a woman? He glances over at me with an apologetic look, but I can't look at him. I'm afraid I'll start crying.

Belinda is taking sick pleasure out of this. She's had it in for me from the moment we met. I suppose I only make her job harder. She smiles so big, I'm afraid her face lift might pop out of its placement, dropping layers of loose skin down to her neck like a disturbing scene in a science fiction movie.

'Tomorrow night. We're announcing the whole thing on *The Tonight Show*. Aren't we, kids?' She slaps Taylor on the butt. His eyes move in every direction but toward me. Just in time, Richard comes in from the kitchen.

'All right, everyone, dinner is served. Let's migrate into the dining room, shall we?' He bounces off through a set of enormous French doors into a lavish dining room already set for dinner. If you can believe it, a second, completely different oil painting on Jackie O hangs in this room as well.

We all follow and sit down. I can feel Taylor's eyes staring into the back of my head but I don't turn around. I won't give him that. If I were stronger, and had another ride home, I'd probably storm out right there, but I've got neither of those things so instead I sit.

The table is set in an extremely 'rich person' fashion. All the different kinds of forks and spoons and glasses. I'm already dreading having to figure out what fork goes with what course in the meal, when an arm in a white long-sleeved shirt appears to my left.

'More wine?' a familiar voice asks. I look up. Holy shit! It's Josh.

'Alex?' He's just as shocked to see me, maybe even more so. 'What are you doing here?'

Taylor's face reddens from across the table. Belinda immediately switches into high alert, clearly smelling danger. She shoots Richard a terrified and angry glare, then shoots her eyes in my direction.

'Alex is our client. Who are you?' she asks Josh, her tone immediately threatening. Josh is taken off-guard. I can tell he regrets even speaking on the job.

'I'm very sorry. We just know each other and I didn't know you—' Josh stammers. I feel terrible. I want to do something to stop his humiliation.

'I just signed with Richard's agency,' I blurt out.

Everyone's eyes widen as they turn in my direction. *You did?* they all seem to say. Taylor speaks up.

'That's right. And this is our celebratory dinner. So, cheers to Alex.'

Everyone holds their glass awkwardly in the air and join him.

'Yes, cheers to Alex,' Richard says.

Josh smiles.'Well, good for you, man. Now what Matty told me makes sense. Is this why you might move New York?'

As the words are coming out of his mouth, everything goes into slow motion. I look over at Taylor, whose face is flushed. This was not how I planned on bringing up New York, but finding out he's planning to elope with a supermodel is something I hadn't planned on either. I'm torn between wanting to explain myself and wanting him to feel as crappy as I do.

'Yes, Alex.' Taylor's face has now hardened and his tone has become cold. 'Is it?'

I'm quiet for a moment. I have a few options. The best of which is to run for my fucking life, but I don't do that. I'm nowhere near that dramatic. This is the perfect example of complicated versus. uncomplicated. Here's Josh, simply happy for me and my job as he pours more wine, and directly across from him is Taylor, sitting next to the woman he's going to marry so he can get a big *People* magazine cover story in a few weeks.

For the first time, the ball is in my court. I don't want anyone to get hurt, and I'm ashamed to admit it, but especially not Taylor. I want to stand and clear up everything, to Taylor, to Josh, to Richard, Natalie, Belinda, and her bizarrely quiet husband. But instead I just smile, the kind of big, fake Hollywood smiles I've seen on everyone's face all night, and say, 'Yes. It is exactly how I got my job opportunity in New York.'

The room is silent for a moment. You can almost hear Belinda's botox oozing through her bloodstream, killing skin cells.

Finally Richard breaks the silence. 'Well, mazel tov, Alex!'

Everyone clinks their glasses together and fakes yet another Hollywood smile. Looking down at our plates, we all begin to eat with a silent tension that's so thick I could cut it with one of the knives sitting in front of me. If I only knew which one was appropriate to use.

* * *

The rest of the dinner is beyond uncomfortable. It becomes obvious to me that everyone on Taylor's 'team', as they call themselves, knows everything about Taylor's personal life. This would be creepy no matter what Taylor was into, but knowing what I know, it just might be the creepiest thing I've ever witnessed.

Something tells me Richard, his agent, takes a weird pleasure out of imagining Taylor's personal life, and that Belinda hasn't had sex since before the civil rights movement. Natalie is the strangest of all, she seems totally okay with having a secretly gay fiancé who's into BDSM. She's a beautiful woman and it's strange to me that of all the men in Hollywood that are undoubtedly at her door, she'd pick Taylor.

Josh avoids any eye contact for the rest of the dinner. I feel bad, I think he's embarrassed to have been so called out in the middle of everything. Usually when you cater-waiter, you can disappear into whatever is going on, but not when the guy you have a crush on turns up at the home of one of Hollywood's most powerful agents sitting across the table from two of Hollywood's biggest movie stars.

Speaking of said movie star, he also has avoided eye contact for the entire evening. Once the night is over and we're alone in the car, the tension is even stronger. He ignores me in silence for a good twenty minutes until I finally speak.

'Look, I'm sorry. I was going tell you.'

He lets out a 'hmmph' as we turn onto San Vicente. He can't possibly think he's the only who's been lied to here. He can't possibly be playing the victim.

'I have every right to be as angry as you do, y'know?' I tell him. 'Even angrier, actually.'

'Oh, do you?' His words are sharp and cold.

I do. He might not see it that way but I do. Sure, I haven't told him I might be moving to New York City, but that's only because he's the reason I'm considering not going. It's a *much* bigger deal that he's getting married. I don't care if it's a publicity stunt or not. It is *marriage*.

'Were you planning on telling me you're getting married or were you just going to hire me to cater-waiter the reception?' I spit out at him.

'Were you planning on telling *me* you're moving away?' Taylor turns onto Santa Monica Boulevard. 'Or were you just going to send me a postcard?'

I want to shake him, scream in his face until he understands that I will stay for him. That if he'd allow me to be his, his in a real way, not a dom/sub contract way, but an honest, loving, real way, I'd stay—I'd stay for as long as he'd have me.

'You don't understand. If Belinda hadn't said that, I would have explained. I had planned on telling you everything after dinner. That's why I wanted you to meet Natalie first, so you could understand how—'

'Understand what? How gorgeous your new wife is? Jesus Christ, Taylor—'

He pulls over to the side of the road. 'Listen, you know why I'm marrying her—' He flips on his flashers. The flashers tick in rhythm, making a weird spoken-word poem out of our argument.

'Yeah, to sell your next movie!' I want to rub as much salt into his wounds as possible.

'You know that what I do with my personal life is part of my business. You knew that going in to this.'

'But it's selective, only parts of your personal life, right? Only the parts your publicist decides—'

I can feel his anger rising. His face is getting redder and redder. His eyes are crazy with rage.

'So fucking what! Natalie and I aren't even going to live together. We're having a ceremony for photographers then going our separate ways. We'll be divorced by the time awards season rolls around. She knows about us. She wants to be your friend!'

It's too much to process. His *wife* wants to be his gay submissive's friend?

'Do you realize what you're doing? You're a gross stereotype in the long line of closeted movie stars too scared to actually be themselves—'

He ignores my comment and charges ahead.

'When were you going to tell me that you're moving across the country?'

He's good at switching the topic to why it's *my* fault. He knows just how to play his own selfish game. It's infuriating but, dammit, it's also really hot.

'I haven't even decided about that—' I shout back unconvincingly.

'I am your dominant. You make all decisions through me—'

'You are *not* my dominant. I haven't signed a thing. And if this is the way you're going to treat me, I never will!'

We're fighting—we're full on having our first fight. It would almost be like being in a real relationship, other than the fact that we're arguing over his fictional marriage to a woman and a contract outlining a very complicated sex life.

'You're a coward, Alex—'

I'm the coward? *Me*? Not the closeted movie star with a secret sex dungeon?

'You want this ... you want me, but you're afraid. It's the same fear that's kept you a virgin for all this time and it's the same fear that's kept you single! And now I'm here, trying to be with you. Trying to give you all that I *can* give. I can tell you want it. From the moment I first laid eyes on you I could tell you were different from everyone else. That you were curious and open. *That* is why I was drawn to you. So now, after everything we've done together, what is it you're afraid of?'

It suddenly occurs to me that he might be right. Maybe I *am* the coward. Maybe I am running away from this. What Taylor picked up on, the curiosity and openness, he's right. I just had to go and fall for him and screw the whole thing up. Well, why not sign? Why not take the road that's been laid out in front of me? Is it just because I want more or does it go deeper? And will I ever be able to find out if I run away?

'Are you afraid of me, Alex?' His voice is dark, angry, sexy.

Is he just fucking with my head? Is he just trying to get his way again? Or is he actually fighting for me?

'I don't know what I'm afraid of.' Suddenly I feel emboldened. 'What are *you* afraid of, Taylor? Actual connection? Is that it? Because I like you ... no, I love you. For real love you and you know that. And you love me, I can feel it. But you're afraid. Of what I don't know. Your career? Your money? What? What are *you* afraid of?'

Taylor suddenly floors the engine and we speed back onto Santa Monica Boulevard. He makes a sharp U-turn and we now flying through traffic.

'Where the hell are we going?'

He doesn't take his eyes off the road, he's got that look—the same one he had the last time we had sex. Taylor runs a red light and under his breath mumbles, 'You need to stop asking so many fucking questions.'

When we pull into the valet entrance of the Roosevelt

Hotel, I have a sudden sense of what might be in store. I've begun to notice the pattern of Taylor Grayson, and it's that he wants sex in the wake of any sort of conflict. Something tells me he's never said he's sorry to anyhone. It's as if he heard that Ali McGraw line from the movie *Love Story* and really took it to heart: 'Love means never having to say you're sorry.'

But if that's the case, does it mean ... he loves me?

Taylor hands his keys to the valet attendant and we hurry inside. He's not even looking at me, just straight ahead, lost deep in thought somewhere back at dinner in Beverly Hills. We get into the elevator and it takes us up to his floor. The doors open and he charges out into the hall, I follow behind. Why, I think to myself, do I continue to follow this beautiful asshole?

He flings open the door to his suite and slams it behind us. He begins removing his cufflinks and they clink on the glass top of the dresser next to the bathroom. Clink. Clink. Then his shirt, he unbuttons it with lightening speed and hangs it up in the closet. I'm struck by just how predictable Taylor Grayson is. No matter how passionate he might be, he always manages to keep things orderly.

I'm standing by the door watching, quiet, not sure what I'm supposed to do or say. He walks over and takes me by the shoulders. He spins me around and unfastens my belt. He unbuttons the top button and my pants fall to the floor. I'm standing in my grey Calvin Kleins and a pair of white socks with black shoes. Nobody ever said I was a fashion icon.

Taylor next yanks my body into his, and I can feel his

erection against my back. It's growing by the second. He grinds into me once, twice and then a third time, aggressive and fast. He lowers his mouth onto my neck, his tongue moving from my neck up to my ear. He nibbles the top, at first delicately, then hard. I cry out but he stops me by slapping his hand onto my mouth.

'Oh, so now you want to talk, huh?' he whispers into my ear. It's the angriest I've ever seen him and I'm beginning to wonder if I should be a little freaked out or just continue being so turned on that I might pass out.

He takes me by the waist and leads me over to the bed, bending the top half of my body over so that my stomach is lying on the bed but my feet are still on the ground. He pulls my briefs down and the skin of my bare ass prickles from the room's cool air. Before I can even think, Taylor slaps his palm down onto my bare skin. SMACK! It tingles, like when your foot falls asleep during a movie and then you have to walk to the bathroom. Then the tingle moves to a feeling of shock. Then comes the pain, the deep, red, stinging, throbbing pain, and it's intense. I can practically feel my ass reddening by the second as I let out a moan. Just as I do, his hand comes down again, this time even harder, and I cry out again.

He pushes me all the way down onto the bed and I fall into a pile of pillows, which muffle my cries. The cool sheets feel nice on my stinging bare skin.

Taylor pours himself a glass of ice water from a pitcher on the bedside table. He takes a long swig, then joins me on the bed. He straddles me and pins my arms down. Then he he drops an ice cube out of his mouth onto my left nipple.

When it lands, I immediately feel the sharpness of the cold. The cube just sits there, slowly melting on my warm flesh. Taylor watches as my nipple gets harder and harder, and I can tell he's taking pleasure out of it even though he's not smiling.

He reaches for the glass of water, presumably to get another ice cube for my other nipple, but with my now loose right hand I push him off me. He falls over onto the bed and growls something at me, sounding like a werewolf or Kathleen Turner. He tries to pin me down again, however, now I'm in combat mode. Something has snapped. I don't know what's come over me. This dom/sub thing works both ways, and for the first time I'm feeling my own strength.

He reaches over to grab my shoulder but I grab his wrist. At the same time I untangle the skinny black tie from my neck, and while he attempts to push me off him, I tie his right wrist to the bed post. It isn't an easy task as he continues to try to subdue me, but eventually I secure his wrist. I tie a triple knot and for a moment I wonder what my Boy Scout leader, Mr Eberhart, would say.

Taylor grabs me by my ass with his free hand. He smacks it hard but the pain is milder this time. Perhaps it's because I'm getting used to it or perhaps he didn't get as good a swing in. As he swings around for another smack, I grab his free wrist.

He stops and looks me dead in the eye. 'What the fuck are you doing?'

But I don't answer, I don't even acknowledge him. His precious contract states that the submissive cannot look directly into the eye of the dominant. Once I get his free wrist tied, that's exactly who I'll be. His dominant.

I grab the buckle on his belt as he moves back and forth trying to inch himself away from me. I yank again and again until the belt snaps past the last loop of his pants. I remove his pants and underwear. Satisfied at last, I lean back and admire the view—there he is: Taylor Grayson, tied up and at my mercy.

He's flailing about, trying to break loose but he's not going anywhere. I don't know much in life, but I do know how to tie a knot.

I grab the glass of ice water he'd used on me and put a cube in my own mouth. Following his routine, I drop the ice onto his chest where it melts slowly into his patch of chest hair. I get another ice cube and this one I drop onto his right nipple. I press it deeper and deeper into his skin until it melts, his skin tingling from the cold. All the while his face is scrunched into a painful expression and for the first time I really understand the pleasure one gets from being a dominant. For the first time, in maybe ever, I feel truly in control.

I pick up a condom from the dresser and slip it on quickly, willing it not to break in my haste. I spread his legs into a wide V-shape and go down on him—his cock hardens, growing bigger and bigger inside of my mouth. As I suck, I slip my now lubed index finger into his ass. It's tight, very tight. He whimpers in pain and lets out a slow deep breath.

I continue to suck as I slip a second finger inside Taylor, his eyes widening and his moans getting longer and longer.

With my free hand I open the drawer on the bedside

dresser. Inside is Taylor's 'home away from home sex drawer'. There are more condoms, nipple clamps, a silver neck tie and a leather riding crop.

I grab the neck tie and wrap it over his mouth to muffle his cries—also because it looks really hot. I take out the nipple clamp and place it onto his left nipple. As the clamp closes tight on his skin, he lets out a muffled cry. I repeat the process with the right nipple, and Taylor's cries get even louder.

I grab the riding crop, and pull his legs together. He's on his back so I lift up his legs and flip them back so that his ass is in the air. His ass is so beautifully round and smooth. I trace his asshole with my tongue—I know from experience that it's sensitive from the finger fucking I just gave him. The feeling of pleasuring him, of watching *him* squirm is making me harder and harder.

I've never used a riding crop, even while riding a horse, but it seems pretty self explanatory. I swing back and swat down on his ass. Taylor writhes in pain as his skin reddens into a long line, the shape of the riding crop. I watch as the red skin fades to pink. I swat him again, this time even harder. But this is only the beginning.

I lower his legs back down, spreading them open, then with my rock-hard cock I slowly enter him. Taylor's ass is even tighter than I imagined and as I slide my dick in. His hands ball into clenched fists getting tighter the deeper my cock goes. His eyes are open but they're rolled back so far that I can't make eye contact. He's literally whimpering like a baby as I lean my mouth into his ear and trail the inside of it with my tongue.

I whisper, 'This is what happens when you try to turn a master into a slave.'

I don't know what's come over me, but I there's no room in my mind to process it. I'm fully present. I'm right here thrusting into Taylor Grayson. My thrusts get faster and faster, harder and harder, his whimpers growing longer with every thrust. He's covered in sweat by now, and the bed is squeaking and for a moment I think I'm literally going to break it. I grab hold of his hair and yank it as I pound into him again and again. My cock is so deep into him it that it looks like we're connected as one.

I grab his cock, dripping in precum and red with anticipation, and hold it in the palm of my hand, moving my fingers up and down. With each thrust, I give his cock a jerk. His eyes are now closed tightly and he is biting down onto the necktie. I feel like a superhero whose power is his giant throbbing cock, shattering the walls built around the rich and famous.

I'm almost ready to come, my balls and stomach muscles tensing up, but I don't slow down. I speed up, hammering his ass harder and harder. The feeling is spectacular, but every so often little thoughts of his getting married enter my head. I do my best to ignore these thoughts, fucking Taylor even harder. But I can't help but think of his life of lying and the heartache he continues to cause me. I think about how I am worth more than a guy who can't show up—but I wonder if it's possible to feel this kind of heat with someone else.

I snap back into the room, Taylor's body trembling beneath me. I can sense his orgasm beginning and stroke his rock-hard dick up and down, over and over, as my own orgasms rises.

Finally I can't hold back and explode inside him—and just as I do, he explodes as well. He shoots out rope after rope of cum, porno movie-style gushing like I've never seen him do before, it goes everywhere, shooting into the air like darts from a Nerf gun. His body trembles in pleasure as his cum keeps spraying out with no sign of stopping. His warm cum covers his stomach, his chest and anything within a four-foot radius.

As I pull out, I remove the tie from around his mouth. Taylor closes eyes and falls silent. He's in a zone of either pleasure or utter disbelief or hopefully both. The expression on his face is one of shock and exhaustion. I lean down and kiss him on the forehead and just for a moment, I place my hand on his knee. I leave it there for a moment imagining that we have a 'normal' relationship. That we can simply make love to each other without any walls or hang ups. I have no idea what's next but there's a good chance this will be the last time I ever touch his knee again.

I untie his writst and we lie there next to each other on the damp mattress, still catching out breaths. Neither one of us speaks. But the silence feels louder than any noise imaginable. I close my eyes and somewhere in the midst of the sea of silence, I fall asleep, feeling not satisfied but accomplished.

* * *

When I wake up it's morning, and I'm not sure how long I've been asleep. I roll over and find Taylor is gone. I sit up and look around the room, but there's no sign of him. His clothes are gone, even the neck tie that was once around his mouth. It's as if he was never there at all.

I get up and look in the bathroom but it's empty. I open the door to the hallway and peer out. 'Hello?' I call out pathetically. The hallway is also empty except for someone's room service tray sitting on the floor across the way. The euphoria of last night vanishes as I realize that it may have been a goodbye fuck. My feeling of confidence and pride subsides. Had our weird, fucked up, complicated relationship reached its peak? Perhaps by taking control, I've officially closed the book on Taylor forever.

On some level I guess I hoped this might be the moment where he realized that it's impossible for one human to give himself over to another without losing himself entirely. It has to be mutual. The power struggle goes both ways, in the bedroom and out. I thought this would show him that the world doesn't end when you let go of control every once in a while. Maybe it does for Taylor.

I call his cell phone but it goes straight to voicemail. I leave a message.

'Hey, where did you go? Call me.'

But somehow I know he's gone for good. I can feel it. I've violated the contract even if it's not signed, and instead of opening his mind I've killed our relationship. This is it. This is the end for real.

I put my clothes back on feeling rather numb. I want to cry, but I also want to walk away and try to never think of him again. I want him back, but I wish I'd never met him at all.

It‘s here, in this empty hotel room, that I decide it's time for me to go to New York, assuming they will have me. Matty is right, I can't give up my own life for someone else. Especially when that someone can't even give up being in control for fifteen minutes.

I get a cab and head home. Feeling a weird since of closure, as tears flow down my face and my heart breaks into a million tiny pieces, I think, Goodbye, Taylor Grayson. I will miss you.

When I arrive home Matty is there. We've successfully avoided each other ever since our big fight, but now we're face to face. In our living room. With an episode of *Here Comes Honey Boo Boo* paused on the flat screen TV.

'Hey,' I say, closing the door. Matty doesn't even turn around. 'Listen, I'm sorry ...'

'You should be,' Matty says, still without looking at me. I walk into my bedroom, but just as I get to the door he stops me. 'I was just trying to help you. I know how much New York can do for you.'

I feel terrible. Matty's been with me every step of the way and I suddenly turned on him the moment we disagreed. All because I was blinded by someone who has proven, once and for all, incapable of being there for me in any possible way.

'You're right. And I'm sorry. I lost my head. There's been so much'—I can't stop imagining myself tied to Taylor's bed—'so much going on. I didn't mean to snap at you like I did. I know you just want what's best for me.'

We look at each other and the past five years of living

and growing up together flash through my mind. I know that this chapter is ending as well, and while I'm trying to ride the excitement of what lies ahead, it is hard, in the moment, to let go of the past.

'It's okay, I forgive you.' We hug but Matty pulls away quickly. 'You smell like sex.'

I laugh and get up, sniffing myself. Good god, I smell the floor of the Pleasure Chest. 'And that's my cue to take a shower.'

Matty grabs my arm 'You *must* reveal details. As a peace offering.'

I stare at Matty. He deserves something, at least a little story about my past month with Taylor Grayson. I have nothing to hide anymore and no one would believe Matty, even if he told people.

'This can never leave this room.'

He nods, but I can tell he's not even listening—he's just waiting to hear Taylor's name.

'It was who you think it was.'

Matty squeals.

'Oh. My. God. You are like a pioneer, a national hero. You're the Neil Armstrong of people who sleep with closeted celebrities!'

'Not a word.' I tell him, attempting my best Taylor Grayson serious face. 'But for the record, it's over.'

Matty frowns. 'Are you sure?'

The past month's moments with Taylor flash though my mind. I see us in his SUV, I see us in his kitchen making dinner, I see myself tied up to the bed, I feel his lips on mine, and for a split second I wish I could go back. I wish that we could take a piece of it, put it in a box and hold onto it forever like a keepsake.

'I'm sure.'

CHAPTER 21

I'M WRITING AN EMAIL to Alicia thanking her again for offering me the job, when Matty comes running into my room.

'You *have* to come see what's on TV right now!'

'Just a minute. I need to send this email.'

Matty is bouncing around the room like Sweet Brown talking about that fire on YouTube. 'No, it can't wait. Come on!'

I can tell from Matty's hysteria that we've either been invaded by terrorists or that Cher finally agreed to do that Bob Mackey directed *Mame* remake. He drags me into the living room and there, on TV, is Taylor Grayson on *The Tonight Show*.

'And when did you know?' Jay Leno asks, looking as ridiculous as ever. Taylor looks great, of course, and he's wearing my skinny black tie. The same tie that I tied him up with the night before.

'Oh, I guess I've always known. You just sort of have a voice in your head that says I'm gay, and some people choose to listen and some people spend their lives trying to ignore it. And I'm tired of ignoring mine. It's a stupid way to live.'

The audience applauds, and Taylor smiles at them.

'And is there someone special in your life? Or is that too private?' Jay asks, sounding like someone's conservative uncle trying not to say anything offensive.

Taylor laughs, and a small part of me wonders if he's about to bring up the sex swing hanging in his house. 'There is. Someone very, very special. But I'm not sure if he still finds me as special as I find him.'

He looks down at his hands and Jay makes some sort of joke about how clean his nails are. Taylor looks up, directly into the camera.

'But he knows who he is.' For the first time Taylor Grayson looks desperate.

'Well, sorry, ladies.' The audience laughs. 'Taylor, I think all of America is cheering for you right now. That took a lot of bravery.' The audience applauds some more and Taylor shakes his head.

'No, I'm not brave. I'm just tired of holding back.'

Jay takes the show to commercial and Matty mutes the volume.

'Oh. My. God. He's talking about you, isn't he?' Matty can't stand still. 'This is your romantic comedy moment!'

'It's not, though. It's so much more complicated than that,' I tell him, but in my head I wonder if it is. Did Taylor Grayson just do his part to end the complications once and for all? Before I can say anything else the doorbell rings.

'I ordered pizza,' Matty says, getting his wallet.

I walk over to open the door. 'There's a lot more to Taylor Grayson than you think.' I open the door and there he is. Taylor. In the same outfit he'd worn on *The Tonight Show*.

'Hi,' he says. Matty's jaw literally drops to the floor. 'Can I talk to you?'

I'm just as shocked as Matty to see him. I don't know what I expected to happen after that interview, but not this. 'Yeah, let's go outside.'

We walk into the front yard and sit down on the steps of the building.

'You got here fast,' I say, staring down at my bare feet on the cement.

'*The Tonight Show* is pre-taped.'

I nod. Oh, Hollywood, how you complicate things.

We sit there quietly for a moment. The wind blows through the palm trees a little, the night is oddly quiet.

'I'm sorry,' Taylor says. 'For all of this. I know I've made this all very strange.' Strange is an understatement, when riding crops and contracts are involved. 'But my life is strange and up until now I've had to spend a lot of money and a lot of time making sure that stuff is kept a secret.' He's looking down at the ground, and I can tell he's nervous. Something I've never seen Taylor be. 'But I don't have to do that anymore.'

'Do what, exactly?'

Taylor shrugs. 'All of it.' He looks up at me. 'I have weird sexual tastes, I know that.'

'That isn't your problem.' I say. 'Sex is nowhere near your problem. The sex is hot. The problem is your being afraid to let anyone in too close.'

We sit there quietly for a moment. I want to hold him

and kiss him, but it suddenly feels important that I remain strong and follow his lead.

'When I was sitting at the dinner table with you at Richard's the other night, I thought to myself, what am I doing? Am I really going to be that guy who never lets go? Who never lets the world, let alone someone he really cares about, actually get to know him?'

He's being open and vulnerable in front of me, and it's strange to see the most confident man I've ever met have even a sliver of doubt.

'Alex, would you like to go out with me sometime?'

I don't know how to respond. 'Yes,' my heart says but my mind knows Taylor's limitations.

'Like, to a movie or something? Y'know, a date.' Taylor smiles at me and it's the first real smile I've ever seen him give. He places his hand on my knee and leaves it there. I stare at it for a moment, then place my own on top of his hand. I nod, afraid that by saying yes out loud I'll jinx the good fortune. We sit there together, in the glow of the moon and the unflattering light of a blinking street lamp. It is, for the first time, truly romantic.

He takes my chin, sweetly and gently, and brings my face up to his. He kisses me softly, then pulls away. We sit there, our noses touching, staring eye to eye. I don't know about the future, and for once I don't even care, I just sit there staring into Taylor's eyes—feeling loved for the very first time.

'I mean, I still want to spank the hell out of your ass, by the way,' he adds and we both laugh.

'You've got a deal,' I tell him.

Then we sit quietly, looking at the stars, never once removing our hands from each other's knees.

EPILOGUE

IN THE END, TAYLOR'S career wasn't over. Far from it. The closeted male superstar thing is so 2002, and all the world needed was a Taylor Grayson to break the glass ceiling. Once he did it, his career blossomed even bigger than it had ever been before. His next movie was his biggest hit to date, a romantic comedy, by the way, where the guy did end up getting ... the guy.

Matty got a raise after Taylor offered to do the first post-coming-out interview with him for *The Star Report*.

And I ended up taking the job in New York.

We're bicoastal now, and it works for us. As Taylor says, after thirty years of being a forced bisexual, having a bicoastal relationship isn't the worst thing that could happen. Just like sharing coasts, we're sharing control, both in the bedroom and not—and it's working for us. He still ties me up in his secret sex room, but now he lets me tie him up as well.

Oh, and I just sold my first book. It's the totally fictional story of a closeted male movie star who falls in love with a hilarious, handsome, talented, clever, completely likeable young writer. In the end, the actor decides to tell the world who he really is. And in the process, he changes a tiny fraction of a world ready to change—and more importantly—his own life, once and for all.